D0271377

'Like the ancient mariner's, Christopher Osborn's voice compels one to listen to his strange, alarming, and ultimately rapturous story. You ignore him at your peril' – John Ashbery

'Let me say at once that I think this novel very remarkable; it contains some things which seem to me better done than I have ever seen them done before' – Stephen Spender

'Christopher Osborn's *A Sense of Touch* is a uniquely structured, immensely readable tour de force. The book succeeds again and again in illuminating the ambivalent, murky hearts of its many disparate characters. It is immediate, truthful and brilliant' – Peter Cameron

'A very promising first novel' – Iris Murdoch

'A self-confident, well-written and interesting novel by a writer of shining promise – Francis King, *Daily Telegraph*

'Osborn builds an extraordinary symphony of feeling in which the hero's relationships with his watching well-wishers are painstakingly unravelled … if the object of a first novel is to make an impact, Osborn has succeeded memorably – *Daily Telegraph*

'Christopher Osborn's astonishing first novel, *A Sense of Touch*, celebrates tactility, taking great jolting electric leaps between the poles of sacrament and nightmare – *Observer*

'Osborn conveys the pleasurable dread of performance with all the conviction of one who knows it intimately' – Patrick Gale, *Sunday Telegraph*

'This extraordinary, complex and beautifully crafted first novel heralds the emergence of a major new writing talent' – *Time Out*

'Splendid dramatic confrontations and a real sense of a writer finding his voice' – *Guardian*

'Osborn himself has [the] gift of immediacy, an ability to present a here-and-nowness of sight, touch and hearing' – *London Magazine*

'*A Sense of Touch* is at once a serious literary novel and a distinctive piece of writing possessed of a strong erotic core … marks a distinguished debut and is a novel which should attract a wide readership' – *Gay Times*

'Remarkable for the skill with which Osborn handles the omniscient narrative method and the way he hands individual perspectives around the tight organising structure of the concert' – *Oxford Times*

'It is Christopher Osborn's achievement, in a finely written book, its prose honed and disciplined, to bring together in a compelling web not only Robert's interrelating lives, but the lives of a circling cast of planetary influences which touch upon him … "A very promising first novel", wrote Iris Murdoch after reading the manuscript. And a disturbingly compelling one, one might reasonably add of the published product' – *Eastern Daily Press*

UNBOUND

UNBOUND

CHRISTOPHER OSBORN

Arcadia Books Ltd
139 Highlever Road
London W10 6PH

www.arcadiabooks.co.uk

First published in the United Kingdom 2017

Copyright © Christopher Osborn 2017

Christopher Osborn has asserted his moral right to be identified as the author
of this work in accordance with the Copyright, Designs and Patents Act, 1988.

All Rights Reserved. No part of this publication may be reproduced in any
form or by any means without the written permission of the publishers.

A catalogue record for this book is available from the British Library.

ISBN 978-1-911350-07-1

Typeset in Garamond by MacGuru Ltd
Printed and bound by TJ International, Padstow PL28 8RW

ARCADIA BOOKS DISTRIBUTORS ARE AS FOLLOWS:

in the UK and elsewhere in Europe:
BookSource
50 Cambuslang Road
Cambuslang
Glasgow G32 8NB

in Australia/New Zealand:
NewSouth Books
University of New South Wales
Sydney NSW 2052

SCOTTISH BORDERS LIBRARY SERVICES	
Bertrams	11/10/2017
	£14.99

To the abiding memory of my
mother, June, and my uncle, Julian.

LIVE
BORDERS

1

Autumn.

In Castir, despite morning mists and a kind of retiring, penitent look about the trees, autumn is mostly evergreen.

But in London … well, the leaves have clung on and on, and this is, they say, why autumn this year is more fantastic than I can ever remember. The city is buried deep, a dazzling flurry of red and ochre. Even my little garden looks like a magic carpet. When the wind blows we take off, my garden and I, and head for elsewhere.

I like this time of year, the month before Christmas, when the days hardly begin before they die. I like rushing days. This year, the weather suddenly turned cold.

I set off one afternoon, when the sun was low, from our house in Marquis Road.

In the morning I had spent a couple of hours at my laboratory in Archway. I went by bus, though tube is easier. Sometimes I walk. But I like the bus best, even though I have to change at Holloway Road. At this time of year, especially in rush hour, the bus windows often steam up. I can never decide if I love or hate this – other people's hot foggy breath mixing with mine and clashing all around me.

I should add that I am one of those lucky mortals who has, all his life, been fascinated by his work. I am a molecular biologist, and specialise in medical research.

In the lab was MM, whose hair has turned grey. It seems to me that this has happened overnight, but I think for a long time he dyed it. Also his hair was so blond that you might hardly notice grey at the beginning. 'Hello Victory!' he greeted me in his usual hearty way. MM is, I have to say, something of a spent force these days. I kissed him on both cheeks, as I always do, but he twisted his head, so I got his ear on both sides. This was faintly unfriendly on his part, but I took no notice. MM and I carry on exactly as before, as if nothing unusual was taking place. I checked up on developments. We are working on three separate drugs at the moment, all for auto-immune disorders. One of them, for lupus, is particularly promising.

And MM checked up on me. He is genuinely interested in my case, as indeed he should be. If there are any positive changes he always congratulates me and laughs warmly. Sometimes I can't help feeling he would rather hear bad news. But perhaps I'm being unfair. One thing I can't help noticing: nowadays I'm slightly taller than him. In the old days it was the opposite. I stoop a little, as I don't want to shock him. But has he noticed? I have no way of knowing, for he no longer confides in me. He has the same friendly voice, rather high and piercing, but it's not innocent. For him I'm mainly a guinea pig, not much different to the rats we keep downstairs (I should add, sensitive reader, that these are well-fed, lead a happy life, and are never tortured).

MM has lost the amazing freshness he had all those years ago. At that time he seemed completely wild, and his thinking was astonishingly brilliant. His English was not very good but that did not affect the speed of his conversation. Talking to him was like trying to talk to an express train. Yet without stopping he took in what you said. And what *he* said, if you listened carefully, was always interesting.

When I first visited MM's house in Muswell Hill I was surprised by its neatness. You had to take off your shoes when you went in. If you picked something up you had to put it back in exactly the same place. The furnishings were spotless. The carpet was white and there was an ugly glass lamp hanging from the ceiling like a flying swan.

The house was plain and small and nondescript, and didn't seem like MM at all. But he showed me around proudly. He was excited by prices and mortgages and being 'on the ladder'. And I must say, financially speaking, he has done very well by us. He is a shareholder and we have had some remarkable successes. I myself, by the way, am quite a rich man. Our research turns out to be very profitable. But I seem to be less and less interested in money, and give a lot away.

♦♦

Anyway, this morning, quite apart from his grey hair, MM seemed to me shrunken.

I said, 'There's nothing much to report. But shall I tell you all the same?'

'Of course, my friend.'

'Well … this morning, when I got up, my ankles didn't hurt, as they often do. And then I suddenly remembered the name of that researcher, Dr Schmidt, who wrote an interesting paper on multiple sclerosis. Yesterday, I couldn't think of his name. That's all, really. No other changes.'

MM shook his head, and tapped me on the back. 'You are a brave man, Victor,' he said, as he often does.

Notions of bravery do not mean much to me. I went round to see Martha, who is in charge of telo production. Martha is a quiet person. She is efficient and works hard. She is good at carrying out instructions and rarely has an original thought. However today she had an idea about modifying the nozzle on the inhalers. She wondered if it would be sensible to tighten the catch so a little more pressure would be needed. I thought this was a good idea. Taking telo can be very exciting. It can be so exciting that sometimes my finger trembles on the catch. And so, if the catch is too loose it can be difficult to control the dosage. There can be a premature release.

MM stopped me on the way out.

'You're looking well, Victory,' he said. 'But as you know healthy appearance can deceive. We need to be sure, medically speaking.'

'Quite right,' I said. 'Maybe it's all in my own mind. I am excited by the experiment, and that in itself is life-enhancing.'

'If you will allow me I will give you health check.'

'Of course.'

I sat, docile and obedient, while he listened to my chest, examined my eyes and mouth, and took my blood pressure.

'You seem healthy,' he pronounced. 'And no swelling beneath the eyes or around the ankles.'

'Thank you,' I said.

I fetched five canisters and took a taxi home. It is important to put the medicine into the fridge as soon as possible. In London and in Castir I have custom-made fridges which monitor temperature very accurately. Telo has to be kept between minus three and minus five degrees centigrade.

I had a light lunch looking out at my glowing garden. Then I took an inhaler from the fridge and placed it on my desk. I left it there for exactly eight minutes. I settled myself in the most comfortable armchair, closed my eyes and did some deep breathing. My head felt light and clear, and my lungs got into a calm, well-adjusted rhythm. These moments, the moments of anticipation, are very intense. My heart was beating fairly fast. Even now I feel almost as excited as I did the very first time. If I don't do deep breathing my legs start to tremble and my hands become clammy.

I took the inhaler and put the nozzle in my mouth. Outside a breeze was lifting and rustling the leaves. I inhale with my eyes half closed but I like to be looking at something beautiful. In Castir it is the olive groves. There, my study window looks down onto row after row of olives, stretching like an army of silver soldiers to the horizon. The best time to do it is the evening, when the neat lines begin to melt into blue shade. Here in London,

I watched the play of leaves in the garden, and held the nozzle gently between my lips. Then I pressed the catch three times, taking ten breaths between each. Telo has no smell or taste but the vapour is cool. We add a little eucalyptus, which clears and opens the bronchial passage. Afterwards I closed my eyes and fell into a doze. I was so perfectly relaxed it was as if I was melting.

♦♦

It was such a beautiful afternoon, so soon to sink without trace, that I went out for a walk. I took St Paul's Crescent and passed the low building, called The Studio, where the sculptor Epstein once worked. Above the studio are two little windows, like black eyes, perhaps a tiny bedroom. I often wonder who lives there, but I have never seen any sign of life. I tried to peep into the studio, but there are gauze curtains which are always drawn.

In Camden Square I waded through the leaves and examined the trees, acacia, oak, ash and chestnut, running my hands up and down the bark. My favourite is a huge plane, on the north side of the square, whose trunk has swallowed up the railing. I feel a natural affinity with these impervious giants, which see so many generations come and go.

Trains pass under the square from time to time, like thunder in the earth. As I walked, scuffling the leaves, I could feel the medicine infiltrating my blood, carried on the red current to every part of my body, homing in like a host of living arrows to the heart of my cells. I always feel, after taking it, a sense of elation, a burst of physical vigour, as if I had just had a drug fix. But this is purely imaginary; telo has no direct chemical effect on the brain. Nevertheless everything becomes astonishingly vivid.

I stood outside the gate of a low redbrick building, set back in an overgrown garden. Engraved on the wall were the words: Foundation Stone laid by A. Conan Doyle in October 1926. It looked derelict and abandoned, yet, in my heightened state, mysterious and alluring. Sometimes when I pass, the gate is open, and dim light comes from the windows. On the gate was a wooden notice, which read:

Spiritualist Temple.
Service Times and Healing Sessions.
What Spiritualism Does.
Provides a Reason for Loving Our Neighbour.
Makes Religion a Reality for the Rationally Minded.

After taking telo I often feel light-headed and restless and wander about for quite a long time. I feel a secret sense of adventure, as if something were waiting for me round each corner. I walked down Camden Mews and peeped in at a workshop where a red BMW was up on a hoist. I remembered the days when I loved driving fast cars and thought I might do so again. Of course these days gas-guzzling cars are quite incorrect, but telo makes one feel irresponsible. If you're not careful telo makes you feel that nothing in the world matters except your own desires. But then, if you think about it, one of those desires might be to do everything you can to help save the planet. Because, with telo, you might have a personal interest in saving it indefinitely.

A mechanic was operating like a surgeon on the BMW and kept flicking his long hair out of the way. He was quite young but already had swollen bags under his eyes. He had an unhealthy look, I could see he drank too much. Alcohol, like telo, eventually affects every part of the body. But while alcohol destroys, telo preserves. I will explain this in a moment. Telo is a big secret, I have never written about it before.

I walked on, under the railway bridge – which is thought, at dead of night, to transport nuclear material – and paused by the American Car Wash Company, run by Albanians. I tried to hear them talking, above the hiss of the wash, in their strange language. I love languages, and speak three. I know two words in Albanian – egg and thank you. I thought of disappearing, changing my name and going to live in Albania.

This is the sort of thing that telo makes you want to do. It makes you want to do it because you are full of hope. There are a thousand possibilities before you and you are invincible. Whatever was smouldering inside you bursts into flame. The flame leaps within you and everything seems possible. Barriers fall like a house of cards.

I crossed Royal College Street and took the little path that curves beside the canal. Across the water I could see a depot of building materials, pipes and flues and blocks of different shapes and sizes. Some of these were brightly coloured and reminded me of the structures biologists use to make molecules.

I watched the autumn leaves fluttering across the depot, settling for a moment and gusting away. The clouds rolled like breakers through the sky and patches of brilliant blue appeared. It was beautiful. Then I realised that behind me, just behind, was a house I knew. I turned round and there it was, number 17 Lyme Terrace.

2

In this house, when I was a boy, lived a girl called Jude. She was a school friend of my sister Pauline.

Let me tell you this story. I am not a writer, and I need practice. I have so much to tell.

One day my sister Pauline, who was four years older than me, developed leukaemia. She was a strong, independent girl, who played tennis very well. She loved animals, and at one time in our little terraced house we had a black Labrador, two wire-haired dachshunds, and an African parrot. My father adored Pauline and could refuse her nothing.

Pauline was sure of herself, full of fun and liked to tease. Her girlfriends often came round to our house, and they made a fuss of me. I was shy and pretended to be off-hand; it was embarrassing to have these adolescent girls drawing me into their games, asking my advice about boys, half serious and half patronising, and then giggling. I was only eleven years old.

Jude had a crush on me. I smile as I write this – I can see her face clearly. She had pale blue eyes and dark curly hair rather like mine. Her cheeks were round and full, and on one of them were two little moles. In our games Jude was always on my side. She came to my rescue when the other girls teased me, and they soon began to call us lovebirds. She called me Victory, which I found flattering.

Once I found myself alone with her in my room. She looked down at me – I hardly came to her shoulder – and said nothing.

I saw her lips part and the tip of her tongue appeared, red and wet, which I found faintly disgusting. Nevertheless 'as a man' I realised what I had to do. I pushed her onto the bed, sat astride her and began fumbling with her breasts. She struggled but I pushed her roughly down and tried to kiss her. She gave me a sharp slap and we both got up, blushing. At the door she paused and put her finger to her lips.

'Don't tell Pauline,' she said.

But Pauline looked at us curiously, and colour rushed to her cheeks. With me she was grumpy and evasive, and she shot angry glances at Jude. I could not quite understand it. Was my sister jealous? Did she love me so much that she wanted me all to herself? It was true that sometimes she took my head in her lap and played for hours with my curls. She was proud of me and showed me off to her friends, saying how cute I was – though I never thought myself cute or handsome.

But now she became sulky with me, for the first time in my life. All her attention was for Jude. And I began to understand. She was in love with Jude.

At the same time she fell sick. My wonderful sister, whose energy knew no bounds, became pale and lethargic. She lost her appetite, for food and for life, and dark circles appeared under her eyes. The mood in our house became sombre. My parents were on edge, tired and strained. A deep unhappiness crept into our lives and filled the house like a poisonous cloud.

I heard the word leukaemia; in secret I looked it up in the dictionary. When I found it, and read about the disease, my fingers became cold and clammy and terrible anxiety overcame me; my sister was mortally ill. For many nights I could hardly sleep and my stomach churned with fear. I began to pray. At night I knelt beside the bed, concentrating with all my strength, and begging God again and again to cure my sister. I knelt rigid, for as long as I could, with all my determination, and I even put nails under my knees, and stones, to placate God with my sacrifice. Now, as I write this, I can almost feel again the cuts and bruises that I inflicted upon my knees and the intensity with which I begged and implored God. And if ever I fell asleep without praying, I would wake in the night with a stab of guilt and immediately get onto my knees, fighting sleep, and remain motionless for as long as I could, kneeling on the sharpest objects I could find.

But nothing helped. Pauline was having chemotherapy, and soon her thick wonderful hair, which was dark and straight, not curly like mine, began to fall out. She covered her bald head with a little woollen hat. I hardly recognised my sister. Her strong arms, which had shown me how to use a tennis racket, which held me and buoyed me up, became limp and soft. Her skin was so pale that it became transparent. On her face the flesh fell away and I was afraid her cheekbones would pierce the surface. She became beautiful in an awful, frightening way. But still she liked to play with me, and sometimes she laughed and teased me like before, and each time I thought: she's getting better. I spoke to God under my breath, and tears of gratitude came to my eyes. But after these games she was exhausted and fell suddenly asleep as if crushed by a great weight.

The weaker she became the more desperately she fell in love with Jude. Jude was horrified by her illness and instinctively withdrew from her. But Pauline's need only grew, and this shocked and repelled her. Jude still fancied me and I used this to try and bring her to see my sister. But Jude did not want to be left alone with Pauline.

One day she let me touch her breasts and laughed, and quickly kissed me on the lips. She said, 'You know, your sister …' and broke off.

'Please, Jude,' I said, 'she loves you so much. Couldn't you make an effort?'

'Listen, Victory, I want to tell you something.' She looked at me with her strange eyes, and I thought with pleasure: there's something wild about her.

She said, 'You know, Victory, Pauline's a lesbian.'

After that I too looked at Pauline differently, for a while. I studied her, and it seemed to me that she had turned into an odd gangling creature, neither a girl nor a boy. The little woollen cap which she now wore all the time also seemed to change her personality.

I said to Jude, 'Don't worry – it's just her illness.'

I was pretty sure it was her illness that was making her into a lesbian. And perhaps the treatment. But, as it turned out, Pauline remained a lesbian. And as she grew weaker she longed more and more for Jude.

◆◆

Once I went with my mother and Pauline to the hospital. While she was having her painful injections I sat in the waiting room. I leafed through an old issue of the *National Geographic* magazine. The bright pictures of coral reefs, transparent oceans and brave young divers delighted me. But then I turned the page, and a shiver of horror and excitement ran through me.

A vast shapeless form, lying on four trestle tables, was spread out on a double page. A man was leaning across it, sleeves rolled up, probing with a pointed instrument. He was tiny compared with the huge thing that lay before him. It was a creature; a blubbery purple mass, streaked over with blobs and white swirls.

As I write this now, I have the picture before me. I am orderly with papers; yet it was a surprise to find that I have kept it all these years. It is a great picture. It reminds me of photos of the earth from space, dark continents and blue seas overlaid with racing patterns of cloud.

I read the caption: 'A colossal squid caught by fishermen in Antarctic waters is the first example of Mesonychoteuthis Hamiltoni retrieved virtually intact from the surface of the ocean. The squid's mantle, or cylindrical body, is one of the largest ever found. With its arms and tentacles stretched out it measures nearly seven metres. Only six specimens of the so-called colossal squid have been found – five of them inside the stomachs of sperm whales.

'Mesonychoteuthis Hamiltoni is an extremely aggressive squid which chases large prey such as Patagonian toothfish. It has the largest eyes of any animal and razor-sharp hooks on the inside of its tentacles which can twist and tear prey to pieces.'

This affected me deeply. The contrast with the sunlit seas of the previous pages could not have been greater. And yet below the lovely surface such monsters were to be found. I was spellbound. For this formless mass, its purple flesh oozing between the trestle tables, had eyes and hunger and purposes, it was a complete living thing, unimaginably different and yet no less real and alive than I myself.

I was alone in the waiting room. Stealthily I tore out the double page, folded it carefully and put it in my pocket.

I knew that my sister was missing Jude dreadfully. And yet Jude was more and more reluctant to visit her. Pauline's conversation was full of Jude, and her eyes shone with an otherworldly light as if a sad ghost had taken possession of her. She told me how they had met in school and immediately knew they were soulmates. 'Has that ever happened to you, Victory?' she asked. 'Do you know what that feels like?'

As it happens I did. For I was 'in love' with a boy I had met in the local playground, a black boy called Vivian. He was a fantastic roller-skater, and taught me how to do it. He could do anything on rollers; he never seemed to lose his balance.

Vivian lived with his foster mother, for his real mother was a prostitute. From time to time he would run back to his mother's house and wait on her doorstep. But when she came home and found him waiting, she did not want him. She kissed him and cried over him but would not let him stay. Vivian always defended his mother, saying she was too busy for the moment to keep him. But soon he would go back and live with her again.

I told Pauline about Vivian and even invented a few details, putting into words one of my fantasies in which, after a daring leap, he fell and hit his head on a bench. For the first time, in my fantasy, I saw him cry and his body was shaking. I lifted him onto the bench and he lay with his head in my lap.

Tears came into Pauline's eyes. 'So you understand ...' she said.

I nodded. I said that Jude was going through an odd phase and was unwilling to spend time with her friends. But in private I was working on her. And when Pauline reached her weakest point and seemed no longer to have any interest in living, I finally persuaded Jude to go and talk to her.

I did not prepare Pauline for this visit. Jude went up the stairs to her room, knocked softly and let herself in. I placed myself outside the door. I was concerned that the meeting might go badly wrong. I knew that Jude could not respond to her passion. I listened with my ear to the door. At first I think I heard my sister's sharp intake of breath, and later a few sobs. But I heard no talk at all. They were sitting in silence; perhaps Jude allowed her hand to be taken? Through the keyhole I could see nothing.

When Jude came downstairs, half an hour later, she was quiet and it looked as if she had been crying. I went up to my sister's room and found her sitting up in bed. For the first time she had a little colour in her cheeks. She was smiling. She gazed at me and I no longer saw the sad ghost. This was the moment at which her recovery began.

Jude's visit had done it. And Pauline never looked back.

Dear old sister! I must try to see you more often.

3

I stood outside Jude's house, which long ago I had known so well. If the door had opened and Jude come out, she would not have recognised me. For Jude would be an old woman now; it was so many years since she had seen me. But perhaps I would say: It's me, Victory, do you remember? She would stare at me in disbelief, with those pale eyes that had something wild about them. And perhaps, because she was a stranger and yet not a stranger, and because she had cured Pauline, and because I would never see her again, perhaps I would say: Jude, don't look surprised, I want to tell you something. Will you listen?

I will try to be as clear and untechnical as possible. I will try to do my scientific best.

I am sure you know something about genes. I expect you know that in each of your cells, in the centre of each, all squashed up, is your genome. In the heart of almost every cell in your body lives your complete DNA, your genes, your blueprint.

I am a molecular biologist. In my lab we have some brilliant researchers, especially MM. Over the years we have had many successes, in particular with auto-immune disorders. One of our greatest successes has been multiple sclerosis. Due to us, the symptoms of multiple sclerosis, in many cases, can be greatly alleviated.

Multiple sclerosis is caused by degeneration of the myelin sheaths, which protect nerve cells. These myelin sheaths are destroyed by the immune system itself, which mistakes them for foreign bodies. The immune system is a ruthless killer, and it makes an error of judgement. A small malfunction of the genes sets it on a course of auto-destruction. By a process of gene therapy developed by my laboratory we can help to correct this malfunction. And so people who could no longer move, or lift the smallest weight, or eat by themselves, people who have lived for years in wheelchairs, in isolation and despair, who have longed to die but lacked the physical strength to kill themselves, these people have begun again to walk, to smile, to laugh – to live.

And all because of a cunning genetic intervention. Small inputs, the right nudge one way or the other, can have momentous consequences.

As we grow older our genes seem to lose interest in us. Genes are mostly interested in the young. They look after us quite well until we pass childbearing age. Then they give us a few more years of health and vigour, for, after all, growing children have to be looked after. Then, as grandparents, we can still be useful, so they keep us going for a bit longer, but without much enthusiasm. Genes only care about the next generation.

But why? What happens to our genes as we get older? We are so used to ageing and gradual decay that the question seems laughable. Time passes, we age; that's just how things are.

But why? What actually happens? Is it just 'wear and tear'? Not likely, because within our DNA there are plenty of repair mechanisms. Damaged genes are continually being repaired. But with age the repair mechanisms themselves deteriorate.

DNA is ordered into chromosomes, long twisted strands, forty-six for humans, which contain our genetic material. These strands have endings, which hold them together and prevent them from fraying; rather like the hard bits on the ends of shoelaces. The hard ends of chromosomes are called telomeres. Now what happens is this: every time a cell divides and replicates, the ends of the telomeres are clipped off; and as the telomeres become shorter, the chromosomes themselves are no longer held tightly intact, and begin to degenerate. As a result the genes no longer perform so effectively. And the new cell is made in a decayed form.

This, in living organisms, is ageing.

But within each of our cells a potential antidote exists for this sad state of affairs. This antidote is called telomerase. Telomerase is an enzyme that repairs telomeres. Telomerase causes the replacements of the telomere units that are cut off with each cell division. Our cells all contain the gene for producing telomerase. But in almost all our cells, this gene is switched off.

In cancer cells, however, the gene for telomerase is switched on, and they divide indiscriminately and indefinitely. Tumour cells have become immortal; and this immortality kills us. Many scientists are working on telomerase in the fight against cancer. If the telomerase gene could be switched off, cancer cells would lose their immortality. This is a promising line of research.

But we discovered something else: how to switch telomerase *on*. We discovered how to maintain telomere length – in non-cancerous cells.

Everybody knows about the genetic revolution. We scientists are told: yes, you can do many wonderful things. One day you may be able to cure cystic fibrosis, muscular dystrophy, Huntingdon's chorea, etc., and you can already help victims of Azheimer's, Parkinson's, lupus, leukaemia and other horrible diseases. Marvellous! But still – shouldn't there be a limit? Is it right to play God?

When I hear this I think of Jim Watson, the discoverer of DNA; Jim Watson, our spiritual father, that great creative soul, who used to say with a smile: the fact is, if we do not play God – who will?

Our most godlike act (and MM played a large part in it) has been this: we have discovered how to switch on telomerase production in normal, non-cancerous cells – and to control this production. As a result the telomeres preserve their integrity, and so the genes remain intact.

How do we do it? We have created a medicine, which I call Telo for short. And by means of a little plastic inhaler the medicine is absorbed into the system.

There are, it is true, other elements in the process of ageing and decay. The patient also needs, for example, to take measures against cell damage caused by free radicals. But telo helps here too. Our cells possess numerous DNA repair mechanisms. These become less effective with age and the shortening of telomeres. But by maintaining telomere length, the repair mechanisms themselves remain effective.

We have shown beyond reasonable doubt: the overwhelming cause of ageing lies in the shortening of telomeres.

Now this is, of course, just a sketchy account, not a scientific paper. But remember this, the greatest excitement of our age: a cunning genetic nudge can have momentous consequences.

As it turns out, the lengthening of telomeres does indeed suspend the ageing process. As the telomeres lengthen, the chromosomes gradually recover their earlier integrity. The new cells are fresher, younger than their parents.

And I have a hunch: will there be an actual reversal of decay – a physical, bodily reversal? Will there be rejuvenation?

◆◆

Nobody came out of Jude's house. No old bunched lady with pale strange eyes. It would have been good to see her. But I was happy. I swung my arms; despite the damp weather no trace of rheumatism. I ran to the end of Lyme Terrace and then along busy Camden Road. The sheer noise of it was enjoyable. I walked briskly up Parkway, past the pet stores where we used to buy food for our animals (now a café), past Whole Foods where health freaks try desperately (at great expense) to feel a little younger.

I turned into Albert Street and stopped outside number 143. It was quite a long time since I had been here. There was a new door, 'distressed' green, with a fan window; and the wisteria, which I myself had planted in a little patch of rubble, now covered the whole facade.

For this, long ago, had once been our house. The present owners, whoever they were, had taken trouble and attached the knobbled wisteria branches to wires right up to the roof. It was striking that such a huge specimen could grow from a square foot of London rubble.

In my day this was quite a poor street and the narrow ter-raced houses were hardly considered desirable. But we lived there happily enough, my mother and father, Pauline and I. On the top floor was the spare room; and there, before I was born, and for a few years after, lived a lodger. I looked up at the top window. I could see it was a child's room now. Stars and a dino-saur were stuck to the glass.

When I was about nine or ten, I found something interesting in this room upstairs. Nobody was using it then, it was full of old books and papers, a storeroom. It was dusty, just under the roof; there were cobwebs, odd objects, bits of broken crockery, and plenty of secret places. Certain important things I used to hide up there – for instance the picture of the giant squid I had torn out of the *National Geographic*. But one day on a high shelf I discovered something else: a biology textbook.

Inside this book were diagrams and equations and words in a strange language that made no sense to me. But there were ten pages of plates in full colour, and these intrigued me. They were pictures of frogs. I looked carefully at these pictures, took the book to my room and studied it at night under the bedclothes, with a torch.

Sometimes the frogs seemed to move, as if they were rapidly breathing in and out. They were laid out six to a page. I was fascinated, and stared at the frogs till I knew them by heart. At first they looked similar, almost identical. But then you could see that the skin markings changed slightly from one to the next; and after four or five pages you might be looking at a different species altogether. I tracked this sequential change in detail. Occasionally an entirely new factor entered the picture, a tiny curve or a crosshatch of lines, or a patch of shading that wasn't there at all on the frog's skin in the previous image. And other elements grew fainter and abruptly disappeared. The frogs on page ten looked completely different to the frogs on page one, and yet the changes, from one picture to the next, were almost imperceptible.

I tried to read the text but it was in an incomprehensible language. On the flyleaf a name was written in pencil: Andres F.

One day when my father was out I showed this book to my mother. For a moment she blushed. I don't think I had ever seen her blush before. I observed her closely. She looked at the signature, Andres F., for a long time. What does the F stand for, I asked.

She didn't reply. But then she began to tell me about Andres; our lodger. Our Brazilian lodger who, years ago, studied biology at Imperial College. What she told me seemed almost familiar, as if it had just slipped my mind. She taught him English, she said. And I began to imagine him quite clearly: a studious young man leaving home for his college after a quick breakfast, gradually improving his English so that he stopped consulting the little dictionary he kept in his pocket, sharing our meals in the evening, playing with my sister Pauline and me, and sometimes singing songs in his mysterious language.

He drew pictures too and told us stories. And his stories, my mother continued, recalling the details vividly, were about a little boy who lived in a strange dry place, in a village surrounded by cactuses. At home in Camden Town we had two small cactuses in a pot, but the cactuses in Andres's stories grew in cracked red earth around the village and were taller than a man. The little boy knew that beyond the village, far away, was a great river and his dream was one day to reach the river and travel in a boat to a new land. He wanted, Andres said, to discover a country covered in green grass where it rained gently every day and you were protected from the blazing sun by thick clouds. A country like England, Andres said.

My mother stopped. 'Do you remember that?' she asked. 'Do you remember Andres at all?' I shook my head. 'How could you,' she said, laughing. 'You were only three years old. When he left.'

Later, rummaging one day in her desk when I was alone in the house I came across a little photograph: a young man with curly hair, sharp nose and prominent cheekbones. His eyes are very black and slant to the left. I took the picture to my room. But a few days later I couldn't resist showing it to my mother. I said I had been looking in her desk for writing paper. But she was pleased, I could see that. I didn't have to make excuses. Nor did I have to ask who the young man was. We looked at the picture together, saying nothing, and a pleasant feeling came over me, like lying in a warm bath. Then she looked at me, smiling faintly, as if trying to tell me something.

Later, I began to think about this. Had she loved him, the student lodger from Brazil who left when I was three? Was that the secret she wanted to share with me?

But it seemed to me that there was more, something that touched me personally. Gradually an idea took root inside me: could it be that Andres was in fact my father?

4

My mother died a long time ago.

She suffered from Progressive Aphasia. A disease similar to Alzheimer's. Two years after she died a type of brain stimulation was discovered which slows the deterioration. But that day came too late for her. For a while she was not too badly affected. She forgot names and made odd connections, but she had not lost the sense of things, the sense of what they were. We often laughed at the funny things she said.

But gradually she lost the meaning of words, and then the words themselves. She became completely speechless. After that she did not live long. She went to live with my sister Pauline in Cornwall. Pauline and her partner Rosie looked after her with devotion. Several times she tried to escape. She couldn't bear being a burden to anyone and longed to die. She achieved this one night in her sleep with a big stroke, at the age of seventy-six.

I remember everything about my mother, I could fill a book with the story of her life, of my life with her.

Although she was elderly and ill, her disappearance was unimaginable. For mothers have always been there; when they die, you go out into the cold, cold world. She left us quietly, without pain, without complaint, on an ordinary day, as if slipping into the next room. I knelt beside the empty bed, desolation streaming down my cheeks.

But she rescued me; this is what soon, very soon, even after her death, my mother was able to do. Her spirit entered me on the very day of her death, her love, her trust in me, her strength.

On the day of her death, in the evening, her radiance began to glow inside me, and I was rescued. My grief was transformed.

I write this because I know it is true. I remember it. I repeat it to myself. But now I feel no emotion, no warm tide of tears. My eyes are dry. Sometimes I have a break – as if a corridor, a little pathway to my heart has opened. As I write now this sometimes happens, and I remember with a moment's true feeling. Then I lean back and close my eyes.

People said that my mother lit up their lives. She did this quite unconsciously, unaware of her own radiance. She was the person everybody wanted to be with. I myself used to be a little like this. She sometimes said I was better at it than her, better at understanding different people, at putting everyone at ease. But I was always more self-conscious than her, more posed, much less sure.

When my father and Pauline were out of the house I would get the photograph of Andres and take it to her. But she was not always in the mood, sometimes she brushed it aside. Then I fell into a childish temper; I even stamped on the picture and threatened to tear it up. Because I so much wanted that feeling, the warm feeling I had when we looked at it together, the three of us together.

Once my mother said: He was a serious young man. He thought a lot about everything. Rather like you.

Inside the biology textbook he had written his name: Andres F.

And the F? My mother pretended not to remember. As a ten-year-old I hypnotised her, swinging a watch on a chain. She played along, dreamily following the movement. Andres F, I murmured, Andres *what?* But nothing came of it. Later it occurred to me to ask my father. What was he called, Daddy, the student you once had to stay? Andres, he replied immediately, Brazilian boy. And the F? Ferreira. Andres Ferreira.

My mother heard this conversation. Underneath her powder, which she always used, even at work at the hospital (she was a nurse), because she liked a pale 'interesting' face, I could feel her blushing. 'Did you have an affair with him?' I asked, when still very young. 'Of course not, darling.' 'But you liked him.' 'We had something in common. A way of noticing things.' 'Did Daddy know?' I asked. 'Of course – there was nothing to hide!' But she didn't mean it. She had a way of meaning the opposite. And she wanted me to know it. She wanted me to know that inside her was a romantic world, a hidden landscape, which was not quite satisfied by her daily work and nice, kind, down-to-earth husband. She had a thirst for adventure, for things that were just out of reach. It was this, she seemed to say, that life was really all about. And I knew, already, what she meant. I studied the picture of Andres intensely, hoping I looked like him.

I soon discovered that Ferreira was one of the most common Brazilian names. And so was Andres. There were probably two million Andres Ferreiras in Brazil.

5

When I was a teenager my parents took me on holiday to Rome. My father read from the guide book, and spoke enthusiastically about the monuments and fountains. At the time I found these historical details boring, and my father pedantic.

But later, as a young man, I went back to Rome and it gave me a lot of pleasure. I felt I was close to the heart of some great mystery. And, it turned out, I had a keen sense of history af all.

I liked being by myself in Rome, I liked to feel that countless generations had trod in the very place where I now walked. I liked to wander in Rome and watch the living, so fleshy and full of blood, and yet offshoots, vivid little twigs sprouting from a vast and ancient tree.

In the Jewish Quarter one evening I climbed through a broken fence and sat on a marble slab in the Teatro Marcello. The sunken columns of this ancient theatre form the foundation of a great palace, which now loomed above me. I sat on a cracked slab at the base of the Teatro Marcello and waited for darkness.

Fierce little cats streaked away and hid. As night fell they cautiously approached and observed me from a distance. In the moonlight I saw that I was surrounded by fallen statues. Moss and tough grass grew among broken stones that were fragments of noses, ears, lips and coils of hair. Pediments jutted from the earth, marble acanthus and ram's horns half hidden in oleander and rosemary bushes. Distant clocks sounded the hours.

I sat among the cats and fractured columns and the antique world rose up. I seemed myself to be carved in stone. For a little while as I sat there in the Teatro Marcello time itself seemed to have no importance at all.

It was then, I think, that the idea first occurred to me: to live for ever, like the sculpted stone around me.

It might be possible to do this, in a half-hearted way, through the imagination. But that was an age-old trick, of little interest. People were always trying to imagine themselves into the past, into nature, or into 'the cosmos', and then pretend they felt better, part of something bigger, etc. I'm not denying that there was something to be gained from these imaginative attempts; but I was thinking of something much more concrete. What I was thinking about was not a palliative.

As a biologist I had an inkling that the rapid degenerative processes of the body were not inevitable.

For the body, a complex, subtle machine, carries within each of its cells the potential for repair. All it needed was a little help – from us. We scientists needed to find a way of stimulating this repair, assisting it, much as a clever medicine assists the body's own defences in fighting illness. This was not a new idea; but until now nobody had known what to do about it.

◆◆

The years passed. I set up my own research lab in London, and we made some important discoveries. I became quite famous in my own field. But my belief that an effective anti-ageing drug was feasible never left me. And I never stopped working on it.

My most remarkable colleague was MM, a young researcher from Russia. When he first came to us, after a year in Hamburg, I thought he was the most unusual person I had ever met. Already a qualified doctor, he had written a brilliant thesis on trace metals and their absorption in the human organism. He was pessimistic about human health, believing that the long-term effects of pollution and additives would be grave. He was a rigorous scientific thinker, yet at the same time religious, often using the word God.

Most amusingly, he believed in reincarnation – he remembered many of his previous lives and would sometimes, after a few drinks, recount them in detail. His voice became shrill, his neck scrawny, and his head strained away from his body, which made him look like a puppet.

Among other people he had once been Akira, the mistress of a Mongolian chieftain in the time of Tamerlane. This was the life he recalled with the greatest pleasure. When the Mongolian hordes stormed westwards, in the fourteenth century, sacking villages and raping women, he was snatched as a young girl from his village in the Urals by a fierce warrior and set on the back of his horse. He then knew a year and a half of tender passion till his warrior was killed in battle in the town of Vladimir.

There were pauses in his stories, during which I tried to bring him back to the present. For I did not altogether like this mystical side of his, which made me think I had engaged a madman to work with me. Dear MM did not mind my down-to-earth interruptions. He was not like a sleepwalker whom it is supposed to be dangerous to wake in mid-flow. As he spoke his round blue eyes stared into the distance, reliving every moment, until, suddenly returning to the present, he burst into high-pitched laughter. He had a wide smiling face like a Russian doll, big teeth and sandy hair.

I think there was not much difference, for him, between past and present. He had a long view of life. He was not much bothered by the passing of days, the continual extinction of weeks, months, years.

◆◆

He said to me once: 'You see, Victory, people long ago feel exactly the same as us. Some things are different – places, habits, aeroplanes, smartphones – but feelings are same – hopes, disappointment, fear, truth, lies, love, happiness, misery. Et cetera.' (MM had recently learned et cetera and used it a lot.) 'We same as them. We are just like them. In fact *we are* them. And future too. We same as future people. We are future people. Time not important, past, present, future, not important. All same.'

MM stepped very easily into the minds of other people, even those from the distant past. And this gave him a remarkable attitude towards life, a remarkably positive attitude. Although he worked hard and enjoyed making money, he could easily shift gear and see things from an entirely different perspective. He really believed it when he said: *we are other people.*

He went on: 'Of course we all like making money, having success, et cetera. This is asserting of self, putting self forward, succeeding as an individual. But there is something else, perhaps more interesting. The opposite of self-asserting. What could we call it?'

I suggested 'self-transcending'.

One day he didn't come into work. The next morning he appeared at nine thirty as usual. I asked what he had been doing. He replied, 'Sorry, Victory. You see my sister in Moscow unhappy. Long story. Yesterday I think so much for my sister. Look, my face – tears.' Thinking about somebody could be, for him, a completely absorbing occupation.

He said, 'Human mind very complicated, Victory. I like your idea, very good phrase – transcending of self. That is correct, I think. Self-asserting and self-transcending. We are both all the time. Very important to understand, we both selfish and opposite, all the time. Like love for example. Love is both selfish and opposite, don't you agree? Must accept it and not be upset. This is human nature, everybody. Selfish and generous all the time. Is not hypocrisy, not at all.' He paused. 'Some people would call this fight between good and bad, but better I think to say – fight between good and good.'

'A fight between good and good?'

MM beamed at me. He said, 'Exactly! The good fights the good. It is fight, but should not be. Quite pointless – but very human.'

'What do you mean?'

'It is simple. Like all animals we are self-asserting. We want the best for ourselves, and try to get it. That is good. But the self-asserting drive, you know, is a hurricane. It can destroy everything else.'

'Yes, I agree. It is overwhelming.'

'Too overwhelming. Because inside us humans is also the other thing. Something we have to look after very carefully. Something important. It is like little candle flame, easily blown out. We have to nurture it.'

'And what is that?' I asked. Although, of course, I knew what he meant.

'Your phrase is good, Victory – self-transcending. That is the other thing inside us. That part of us is not interested in ourselves, but in others. We have both these parts inside us, all the time: self-asserting and self-transcending. It is not either/or. It is and/and. And both parts are vital.'

'Yes – but can we balance them? Can we have them both?'

'Oh yes, we can. We have to. If not, we are doomed. All of us.' MM's blue eyes danced merrily across the rows of pipettes and petri dishes. 'Doomed!' he repeated.

I asked him why we were like this, where such a complicated state of affairs originated.

He replied immediately: 'Mirror neurons.'

'Mirror neurons?'

'Yes, recent discovery. We have special neurons at front of brain, which reflect feelings of others. In this way we are connected to everybody else. Like it or not.' (Another expression MM had recently learned.) 'Of course we think of ourselves, but we need others too.'

'And this is the work of mirror neurons?'

He said, 'Probably. In my own case, I think mirror neurons

work well. For example, my sister in Moscow tells me what she is suffering, and I too become sad. My mirror neurons very good functioning.'

I nodded sympathetically.

6

As I grew older, I began to suffer from an embarrassing condition: impotence. Naturally I found this very distressing. I continued to make love to my wife Lucy, but it was becoming more difficult. I had always been satisfied with my sexual performance; but now my penis no longer bounded forward with youthful excitement. Only half aroused, I had to take hold of my organ with my hand, and insert it, a little roughly, inside Lucy. Then I moved as usual, and she seemed satisfied, as far as I could tell. But, to tell the truth, I was relieved when it was over.

In addition, I often had a nagging headache, sometimes acute, at the back of the head, and a ringing in my ears when I lay down. And my mind was becoming noticeably less sharp, my memory often failed me. It is of course normal, I knew, for people at sixty to forget names, to be a little slower at certain types of calculation. But still.

One day, my heart beating anxiously, I put my own name and number into my address book. And my name, as I wrote it, looked strange, as if it didn't belong to me.

Another day, at the lab, I was making a list of my employees. When I came to MM's name I hesitated. After all he was, had always been, just MM. As I tried to remember MM's name I was aware of an aching pain at the top of my spine, as if an iron bar lay across my shoulders. And every moment it seemed to get worse; every moment, every second passing, the chain around me grew tighter, my ability to move, to live, to think, seemed to fly away; every second was time lost, every tick of my watch drew me closer to incapacity. It was the first time in my life that I realised fully, as I sat at my desk, that oblivion was unstoppably approaching.

Dragging myself stiffly from my chair, I got up and fetched a glass of water. As I swallowed it 'Misha' hit me like a hammer blow. Relieved I hurried back to my desk and wrote it down. Misha M. But then I stopped. What on earth was the other M? Medvedev came to mind; I tried it, but it didn't sound right. I drank some more water and waited. Nothing happened. Medvedev, Medvedev, I murmured, beginning to sweat. Like a guardian angel MM appeared behind me.

'Ah there you are,' I said. 'By the way how exactly do you spell your name?'

MM obliged.

'Makarevich,' I repeated. 'Of course.'

It was time, I realised, to try out the drug I had been dreaming about for so long. The results on mice had been encouraging, but when I started to take it myself I had no idea what the effect would be.

◆◆

It seemed correct that we ourselves should be the first guinea pigs. I suggested this to the three researchers most involved in the project: MM, Vaslav, and Lavinia, my assistant.

I think for a time MM thought of me as a father, and I loved him as a son.

But when I asked him to take part in the experiment he said he was not ready, not brave enough, and it was perhaps, he was not quite sure about this, against his beliefs. The whole thing was very dangerous, he told me. Reluctantly, he would have to say no.

On the other hand Vaslav, a young Polish scientist, and my

assistant Lavinia were at first enthusiastic. Then Vaslav said that, at twenty-eight, with his life ahead of him, he felt he was too young to undertake something so radical. Old age and its problems were far away; perhaps at a later stage, if the therapy was still available, he would consider it.

Lavinia wrote me the following letter:

Dear Victor,

As you know I have been involved in the telo project from the start, and I think I have been almost as excited about it as you. For some time now I have been wondering if I would be one of the first 'guinea pigs'. My children have grown up, and I am well aware of my age and the alarming way in which each day seems shorter than the last. I am still healthy and my work, as you know, fascinates me. The idea of prolonging life indefinitely – as long as it is healthy – has always been the great dream of mankind, and the fact that we now stand on the brink is thrilling and intoxicating. If the experiment works, human life, our concept of ourselves, our place in nature, our entire psychology, will change for ever. Of course I am frightened by these things. But nevertheless, out of fascination for our work – the extraordinary momentum of our project – and also out of solidarity and admiration for you, Victor, I decided to take the leap. The life of middle-aged people tends to become so repetitive, so predictable – despite a comfortable life, a good husband … what does one have to lose? Perhaps I have had enough of 'satisfaction' … I decided to take the leap into the dark, into the future, with you.

But, my dear Victor, the fact is – my husband George will not allow it. I have done my best to persuade him, but he will not budge. He conjures up appalling images of my transformation – he is sure I will turn into a monster, and anyway, he says, I will certainly become a monster in his eyes. He could not possibly want to sleep with me, or touch me, for I will be, he says, an *alien*. If I do it he has no doubt at all that he will have to divorce me. Poor George! He is old-fashioned of course, but I have to take him seriously. He says such a thing defies the laws of nature and gives him the creeps as nothing has ever done before. He talks of 'hubris' and says 'above all we must know our place'. Of course you and I have been through all this, we have weighed the dangers, we know exactly what they are, and what we think about them.

But George will not budge and so, dear Victor, I cannot accompany you on your great adventure. You are brave – you are one of those who believe that as scientists we must do all we can to lessen human suffering. But I do sometimes wonder if you have really thought through the step you are about to take. Have you considered the odd, isolated position you will find yourself in? How will you feel towards others, and they towards you? And what of the serious risk of cancer, among other side effects?

If you turn back now, at the last moment, I will certainly not consider you a coward. Whatever you decide I will support you, I will go along with you, in friendship and admiration.

Lavinia

However, Lavinia changed her mind again and did try the therapy. And George did not divorce her. But I must record a tragedy: seven months later she developed galloping cancer of the bone, and died.

7

I myself took telo for the first time in Castir, our little house in the South.

Among my papers I have found an old account of that day, written at the time. Here it is:

I sit at my desk in a room of medium size, with windows to the south and east. This house stands at the top of a steep village. We have a walled garden, with fig trees and almond and walnut, and a profusion of creeping plants. From the garden a path leads to the remains of a small amphitheatre, set against the hillside. Sometimes we organise music concerts here – the acoustics are perfect.

It is six o'clock. I go to the window and raise the blinds; the Mediterranean evening fills the room. Below, in all directions, olive groves roam to the horizon. I am sometimes disappointed that the trees are planted in such orderly rows, just the same space between each, so that the gentle hills appear scored like grids. But I have only to go to the other window; from here the mountain rises, and the wilderness of Castir.

Castir is a protected nature reserve. To me it is sacred. It is a wilderness I love; I walk there every day and sometimes I seem to know all the twisting paths, all the rivers and streams, to have explored every outcrop and every inch of the mountain; I have spent nights out there, and heard owls and nightingales, and the trampling of boar.

But so much still remains unknown; if I were to wander

all my life I would never discover all the secrets of Castir. On familiar paths I see openings in the undergrowth, which to my amazement I have never noticed before, and these lead me to new places, waterfalls and narrow valleys, where, I sometimes imagine – wrongly no doubt – no other human being has ever set foot.

Now I leave the room and walk down the small staircase that leads to the rest of the house. I pause at the door to the kitchen, half open, and watch Lucy, my wife. Her hair is gathered into a blue and green band and flows down her back. She wears an apron. Her sleeves are rolled up. She is chopping mushrooms on a wooden board. We were surprised, when we went into the village this morning, to see a basket of fresh, perfect boletus in the market. The mushroom season has started early this year. Soon the park will be full of ceps, parasol, chanterelles and devil's nightcap. In season we eat mushrooms almost every day. Lucy cuts the boletus stems into tiny cubes and the caps into thicker slices.

She has not seen me. She goes to the oven, bends down and looks inside. I can smell tomatoes, garlic and olive oil. I have lived with her for fifteen years. Before, I was lonely and anxious; when I met her, from one day to the next, my life changed. In those days she looked almost like a boy, lithe and slim; but underneath, her body was soft. It was a combination I loved. Her shoulders were the most beautiful I have ever seen. I liked to keep her shoulders covered, for I wanted them to be a secret.

Lucy is much more open and honest than I am, and yet the essence of her eludes me. This elusiveness is always present in her face, her eyes, her voice; it fascinates me. Yet she seems serene. I am very lucky, because I think this must be the dream of every man. I am restless by nature, but she is serene.

She still has not seen me. As she bends down and looks in the oven there is a slight stiffness in her movement. Her body is a little thicker than it was, her face broader. She has a few wrinkles around the eyes, and the skin on her hands and neck is looser.

These small signs of ageing touch me. Trees grow more beautiful as they age; why not human beings? I have not told her yet
about telo.

I tiptoe back upstairs. I enter the study and close the door.
Here, along one wall, there are bookshelves to the ceiling. I
am a great reader, and there are books in English, French and
Spanish. On the other walls are pictures, and the furniture, my
desk, the sofa and an armchair, are old and peaceful. Beside my
desk stands something else, white and glossy: a refrigerator. This
refrigerator is high-tech, made to careful specifications. I take a
key from my desk and unlock it. Inside there are several contain-
ers, and two inhalers, or aerosols, like those used by asthmatics.
I take out one of these inhalers and fetch Dante's *Divine Comedy*
from the bookcase, a beautiful edition in English. I sit in the
leather armchair by the window and open the book at the first
page.

'In the middle of my life I found myself in a forest dark
For the right way was lost.'

Yes, so what is the right way? What is the aim, the 'telos' of a
man's life?

I chuckle, I am hardly in the mood for speculation. In my
hand I hold the little aerosol, a common pharmaceutical object.
It is light, almost transparent, made of plastic and titanium. My
hand is clammy and trembles. I close my eyes, insert the tube
in my mouth and press the catch. I have difficulty with this,
my fingers are shaking. I take five breaths. Immediately I feel
my heart beating to burst and my face flushes. This is a psy-
chological not a physical effect. The gene stimulator enters the
blood through the walls of the lungs with no measurable side
effects. The spray is cool and has a faint tang of eucalyptus. I feel
the fresh vapour in my bronchial tubes, almost tickling. This
internal tickling is suddenly intolerable, I explode into a fit of
laughter and then painful coughing. My breath comes in hot
quick gasps, and with my free hand I grip the arm of the chair.
Sweat runs into my eyes, I have difficulty controlling myself.

The vapour permeates my body, to my fingertips, my toes. I lean back in the chair, force myself to breathe deeply. Little by little my heartbeat quietens. I notice the musty smell of books and open my eyes. I am struck by the glow of the fading light, the ochre walls, and the world beyond my window, the ordered olive groves, the amphitheatre and the looming mountain. All this enters and fills the room, as if witnessing my act. I am still trembling. I press the aerosol button two more times, close my eyes and wait.

At last I leave the room and quietly close the door, my legs slightly unsteady. I am not sure what to tell Lucy. But I feel a mighty surge of love and run down the stairs, almost falling. I rush into the kitchen and hug her. She is busy cooking and pushes me away. I feel very hungry and tell her the house is full of marvellous aromas.

8

I did get cancer. A few months after starting telo, I felt a hard little nugget just under my right nipple. Breast cancer in men is rare, but I was fairly sure what it was. In my case the cancer was caught early, and the surgeon decided he did not have to remove the lymph nodes.

It was a turning point. I could have decided to take no further risks and return to 'normal' life. I had a successful career and could anticipate mellow old age with a marvellous woman at my side. I would spend more and more time at Castir, go for long walks and contemplate nature. My gradual dissolution would be sweet.

But, as it happened, I gave this option no more than a passing thought. I had only recently started telo; there was no question of giving it up.

As I lay in hospital after the operation I was overwhelmed by well-being.

Everything around me was so vivid; the glass by my bed, the blanket, a bowl of fruit, the sky beyond the window. And Lucy sat with me in the hospital, day after day.

Certainly, as a scientist, I can explore the endlessly intricate workings of nature. But existence itself, the fact of existing, is beyond the reach of investigation. Every scientist knows this. But for me it was precisely the point beyond which *one cannot go* that I began to see in everything around me.

Why is there something rather than nothing?

To myself I called it the '*yes of course, but –*' aspect. Everything became 'yes of course, but –'. And wasn't that wonderful?

My mind had never been so sharp, and all the odd logic of existence, the all but inextricable web of cause and effect, lay spread out before me. I had a vision of completeness. And all these things were both comprehensible and utterly strange; they all had the 'yes of course, but –' aspect.

I have to admit that, while I was in hospital, another preoccupation kept nagging at me: would I be in time for my fortnightly dose? This anxiety sometimes obscured all else.

But, as it happened, I was released from hospital in plenty of time, with a few days to spare.

When I returned to Castir, every tree, every blade of grass, every patch of moss was a miracle, granting me a glimpse of eternal mysteries. Enough to make you believe in God! I have always been an atheist, yes of course, but ...

Castir, the great natural park which I loved the first moment I set eyes upon it, seemed vibrant with a force which was not just the lives of the animals and plants and trees that lived there, but the life of the rocks and soil and rivers, and all these things together; and the shape of the mountain, the way it rose up against the sky, and the light which bathed it, palest in early morning, blinding in the summer noon, visionary in the evening; by starlight heaving with the song of cicadas.

And I was animated, again and again, by this limitless presence; if I could recapture it at other times, in London or elsewhere, when I was working in the lab, if I could recall it, even the chores of daily life would become good, desirable, for they seemed to be in the service of something great, something that made existence, in the end, worthwhile, despite all the suffering.

It was Castir, more than any other place I have ever known – except Rome? – that brought me close to this greatness, to the immeasurable; sometimes out of reach but sometimes – often – walking there, or even thinking about it, I breathed a richer air, and was filled with a sense of depth, the sense that things are more than they seem. As if a monochrome world is revealed as a place of light and shade and colour, and the colour is endless, and is in everything; so alluring that a smile rises up in you, and you say, you whisper, *yes, I love it* ... for this is the true, the magical face of things. And separation, alienation, sheer boredom – dissolves. This is happiness! The refinding of love for the things that you love, but had forgotten, the people you love but had grown too accustomed to. And the most ordinary mundane things take on meaning – because in fact, despite appearances, nothing is ordinary or mundane.

This magnificent happiness I experienced quite often, especially, I think, after starting telo. In our little house beside the amphitheatre Lucy and I loved each other better than ever before; we were filled with the spirit of the mountain.

9

How did I meet Lucy?

I'm trying to remember the Victor of the old days, it's quite an effort. That Victor was a good scientist, a nervous person who liked music a lot.

I'm trying to picture him sitting in a concert hall in Oxford, the Hollywell Music Room.

Why did he go to that concert? By chance. It was raining and he passed the door. A concert was about to start. He went to his seat and immediately Lucy came onto the stage. He had never seen her before, or heard of her. She was small, and bowed quickly with great suppleness as if she was afraid of getting in someone's way. At first she seemed dwarfed by the shiny black piano, which had STEINWAY AND SONS emblazoned on the side in huge letters. But as she began to play, the piano itself faded away and there was nothing but the music. She played Schubert's last Sonata and in the slow movement old Victor's eyes were suddenly wet with tears, and he went on crying till the end of the concert, and even during the applause. He was very soft-hearted.

After the concert he went backstage and hovered by her door. But he didn't dare go in. Instead, he returned to his car on that cold rainy November night and found that it wouldn't start.

As he waited for the AA to rescue him, he saw her; a slight figure walking by herself, a bag over her shoulder, hunched against the rain, that extraordinary pianist, that subtle artist, unknown to him yet having just revealed so much. He immediately stepped out of the car with an umbrella, afraid that he would frighten her as he hurried up from behind in the night like a bat with flapping wings. I think he tripped slightly as he caught up with her, and she glanced over her shoulder. She looked quickly at him and he saw that her eyes burned with a shy fierce light, even in the dark. The eyes of a startled deer. Timidly she accepted his protection against the rain. As they walked side by side the music still rang in his ears, and he felt excited and yet almost calm, for the music was her, and he understood it and recognised it as if he knew her already. And if he hadn't had an umbrella that night in his car none of it would have happened.

Over the years we organised quite a few concerts in the amphitheatre in Castir and Lucy played in many of them. Once, when she was pregnant, she played Schubert's last Sonata there.

It was hard for us to have a child. Eventually we went to a specialist. It was, said the doctor, a case of 'unexplained infertility'. And so we started on the long road of assisted conception. The third time we tried IVF, it worked.

I think Victor never loved Lucy so much as during the months of her pregnancy. As her belly swelled she grew more and more serene. And this serenity was present in her playing. That was the fourth year we had concerts in the little amphitheatre at the back of our house. She was six months pregnant when she played the Schubert Sonata. As she began the slow movement, the light was fading and the lamp beside the piano enveloped her face and hands in a glowing circle. We in the audience sat silent in the dusk as the stars appeared above the mountain, and in the hushed moments we heard the squeak of bats. Lucy sat very still, her head bowed over the keys, and through half closed eyes Victor watched her curving belly. He knew then as he listened that there was no barrier between him and the rest of the world, between one being and another, between present and past, that human experience was one. And he was loved by the marvellous woman whose fingers were uncovering, in front of us all, the innermost places of the heart.

He was at peace.

Soon after, our child was born, a baby boy, Matthew. He was with us for two weeks; then, one night, he died of a brain haemorrhage.

10

In those early years, when the weather was fine, which it usually was in Castir, Lucy and I sometimes took a picnic basket from the house, and walked up the mountain. We looked for a clearing among the chestnut trees.

In autumn there was a constant pattering, like the feet of scurrying mice, as the chestnuts fell to the ground. In dry weather we made a fire and cooked them in the ash. Lucy laid out food on the rug, and I sometimes took off my shoes and socks and walked barefoot on the fallen leaves. I liked the feel of them under my feet, the mulch and prickly husks. Castir is mostly evergreen, only the chestnuts and hawthorn shed their leaves. I stood beside the trees and pressed my hands on the ribbed trunks.

Once, when we were picnicking, a solitary man wandered towards us through the wood. His shoes were split and his threadbare trousers held up by a string. He smelt of alcohol and unwashed clothes.

Lucy recoiled. But I, filled with the spirit of generosity, offered him food and water. I told him he was in one of the most beautiful places on earth, did he realise? The man ate quickly like a savage and said he was busy, he must be off. It was growing damp, the sun was setting.

I took off my scarf and wrapped it round the man's blotchy neck. Afterwards, Lucy was cross. How could I have given away my warmest scarf, a present, what was more, from her? I am sorry, I said, I did it without thinking. I did it because I was happy. It is so easy, I said, in the Castir wilderness, don't you agree? to feel compassion for the world and everybody in it. And because of you. Because I love you.

I do not think, in those days, that Victor was especially worried about mortality. He liked to talk about the cycle of life and death, the decomposition of bone and leaves and wood, and the new life that was born from them. It is nothing, he said, but a re-organisation; everything is in motion, changing all the time. More than once he told Lucy: With you I am not afraid of growing old. When he heard her play, especially Schubert or Beethoven, he said: This music is still alive, as fresh and true as it was 200 years ago. Lightly, teasingly, he sometimes asked: But will you still love me then? When I am old? She had no difficulty reassuring him – of course she would love him when he was old.

I led her on, that time, through the chestnut grove, where the path climbs more steeply. The light was fading. I took her hand and guided her. I could feel her excitement and the question on the tip of her lips: Where are we going now?

It was not long before we reached our destination. An ancient yew stood before us. Its huge twisted trunk, half rotten, clung to the ground with roots like clawing fingers. 'Look,' I said, 'do you see the berries? Red and fresh – yet this tree is thought to be one thousand years old.' Above us, the needle canopy shut off the last of the light.

I knew she expected me to kiss her, perhaps even lie on the ground and make love. But I was in a world of my own, and stared up at the tree.

'Victor!' she called, trying to bring me back.

I had a moment of anxiety, though I didn't show it. The fact was, I couldn't remember the name of the tree.

'Do you know what this tree is called?' I asked her.

'A yew,' she replied.

'Yes,' I said. 'The yew has magic properties. We're working

on an extract from the bark. And something in the berries.' I squeezed her hand.

When we left the tree, the first stars were already out. We knew the way well, there was no danger of getting lost. I was cheerful, and put my arm round her in case she was cold.

I said, 'Trees grow more and more beautiful with time, don't they?'

11

I have a camper van. It is called a 'Cayman Cruiser', and I have parked it, more or less permanently, in the car park halfway up the Castir mountain. It is a modern vehicle, state-of-the-art, and now I often work there; there is a reliable Wi-Fi connection, and I keep in touch with the lab in London. Sometimes, especially in spring or summer, I even sleep there, unwilling to abandon the beauty of the mountain. And I love the night in the wild.

Winter has come and gone. It is the month of April, and in our little garden the first cherry blossom is already out.

I'm in the Cayman now. It's a high-tech creation, with bunk beds, a kitchen, and lots of gadgets. There is plenty of electricity. But for writing these notes, this diary, I light the little oil lamp that we used to put out on the terrace at the house in the old days. For one thing, I don't want to use up the Cayman's battery. But also there's something immemorial, timeless about an oil lamp. It's alight now, on the table in the kitchen, and gives off a pleasant hiss.

It is night. I look out of the window of the Cayman into the darkness of the mountainside. In the valley are countless creatures, Lucy is in her bed at home, life visible and invisible is everywhere. All doomed uncomprehending to decay and extinction.

I stand up and open the window of the Cayman. As the fresh air pours in, I seem to grow. I rise higher and higher, as if my legs were stilts. There is a crescent moon, so clear, so bright! I feel perfect, clear, bright, like the moon, perfectly mineral.

◆◆

There was no proof that telo would stop my memory deteriorating. Never, in my hopes or dreams, did I imagine that soon (how soon? I am not sure) the change would be so dramatic.

I remember each detail of that day when MM's name slipped my mind. I panicked, I sweated, I was engulfed in fog. A poor little man with white hair in confusion. MM appeared behind me wearing a green sweater and a shirt with scuffed collar. There was compassion in his round blue eyes.

I remember, too, the moment with Lucy when I forgot the name of the yew tree. A common name – yet I couldn't find it.

But all that is the past.

My memory now is as accurate as a surgeon's scalpel. Today I could no more forget MM's name than my own. Or any other name. My mind is a huge library and I have access to all the books. My access is immediate. Each book, each reference calls forth another. I could be submerged in an avalanche of facts and cross-references. By writing this memoir I am imposing order, chronology, I regain control.

A good memory is essential; without it, our aspirations, all our actions, become ineffectual. We are shrouded in mist; our best intentions trail into insignificance, and we cling to the few certainties that remain.

I can say with confidence that, since starting telo, my life has considerably improved. I am able to focus more clearly on the things that really matter to me, things I have always believed in. I have become, you could say, more 'myself'.

Our work at the laboratory continues to make progress, and we are closer than ever to untangling the intricacies of the immune system. This gives me hope for the victims of auto-immune malfunction, and there are many of them. Even cancer sufferers may derive benefit, for a strong immune system is the best protection against this disease.

With my sharp mind I am better at detecting 'blind alleys',

directions of research, which I see very soon will lead nowhere. I am more creative at imagining new strategies, inspiring our scientists to explore paths that might never have occurred to them. Think laterally, I tell them. Never fear to abandon tried and tested methods, however hard you have been working on them. Successful ideas often come from a small shift in thinking; even, sometimes, by accident.

I have set up a charitable foundation, to which I have contributed a considerable part of my personal savings. I intend to work closely with Oxfam, Actionaid and other NGOs.

I have always been aware of human suffering, and tried to do what I could. But now, with the help of telo, I have far more energy, and can be more effective. I am happy to say that my capacity to empathise with the needs of others has grown.

Perhaps that is why I feel closer than ever to Lucy. And I am more sensitive than ever to her piano playing, and to the beauty of music in general.

12

I went back to London, to check up on the lab.

MM greeted me with a hearty kiss. He looked at me closely with his china eyes, and said, 'How are you, Victory darling? Any developments, any problems?'

'I feel well,' I replied. 'No rheumatism this year. Above all, my concentration seems to have improved. And I have no difficulty remembering names.'

'Very interesting,' he said.

'I no longer have to write things down. Like I used to, remember? Now it's all stored in here.' I tapped my head.

'Good news. That is progress! So will you write a paper?'

'A paper?'

'Yes. The time has come. Let us publish.'

I smiled at him. 'Perhaps you're right,' I said.

But, though I hid it, I found this a little irritating. After all, I was the guinea pig; it was up to me to decide. Not that I had anything against MM; he was my colleague, my helper, and I had always felt close to him. I loved his brilliant mind, his happy, carefree attitude.

Now he let loose one of his guffaws of laughter.

'If it makes you feel better,' I added.

'My friend,' he said, 'I have been concerned. And I am so happy to see that we are in agreement.'

'All right,' I said. 'You know I always give in to you. I will write something.'

And why not? It was my job as a scientist.

'Good.' He approached with arms outstretched, as if to hug me. But I held back.

'As you, know,' I said, 'our research on telomerase is already patented. And we have received funding.'

'I am not concerned with funding,' he replied. 'But now we have reached the correct stage. It is our duty to publish.'

◆◆

MM was right, of course; it was time. More than a year had passed since I started taking telo.

I decided to release the information slowly. In the first paper I would merely describe our work in the laboratory. At a later stage I would write about the experiment on myself.

I was in good spirits.

MM winked at me and said, 'So the medication is working. No side effects?'

'None at all. Apart from that spot of cancer, which was easily dealt with. Teething problems – inevitable. And I will, of course, have regular check-ups.'

'Are you sure?'

'Quite sure. I feel better than ever. Like an artist,' I added.

I really didn't quite know what I meant by that. But MM nodded as if he understood.

I said, 'MM, do you ever think about your past lives when you work in the lab?'

He replied, 'Well sometimes they pop up in middle of experiment. Usually very friendly. And then I laugh, but not too loud, or others think I am mad. Yesterday I made special probe, red probe, for Cyp2d on rat chromosome 7. And then I saw old woman in Moscow with red hair. Not much hair, but red! And eating *tvorok*. You know *tvorok*? Type of yoghurt old people love.' He winked at me again. 'I have many nice people in here [he tapped his head] and some horrible ones.'

I was just about to ask about the horrible ones when he said, 'How's Lucy?'

I didn't answer straightaway. The fact of the matter was, Lucy had slipped my mind. The word Lucy gave me a little shock, like an injection. I almost said stupidly: Lucy? What about her?

But I recovered quickly.

I said, 'I haven't told her, you know, about the experiment. I can't quite do it yet. I don't think she'd approve.'

MM's eyes bored into mine. He said, 'You can't do it? I'm surprised. Tell her, Victory. You love her.'

I laughed. The fact was, why should I tell Lucy? She had nothing to do with my work.

'Don't forget,' MM went on. 'Whatever you do, don't forget. You love her.'

'Oh, I could never forget! Surely you know that?'

'Of course I do.'

I said, 'My dear friend, you have been close to us for a long time. And I must say that the three of us have lived so many happy moments together, for instance when you come to Castir and we walk together all day on that wonderful mountain and then go back home to a delicious meal in the evening, especially when the wild mushrooms that Lucy cooks so well are in season. And the chestnuts.'

These memories were giving me an appetite. I continued, 'As you know in the course of time relationships evolve. Naturally I love Lucy. But now we are both more mature, more independent. These things happen, it's nothing to worry about.'

MM's emotions are like the emotions of a child. I thought his eyes were going to fill with tears. I studied him closely. He opened his mouth, and was about to say something. But, perhaps for the first time ever, he seemed lost for words. I smiled at him. And then I had a little internal pang, a pang of anguish. Were we no longer, all of a sudden, quite so close? At the same time I felt an odd little rush of pleasure, almost glee, and something inside me said: But all this is so interesting!

I went on smiling and continued, 'I am changing, of course. What do you expect? Perhaps nothing will ever be the same again. But isn't that the point of our research?' As I spoke I wondered if there was any difference in my voice. 'That is, after all, what you and I have been working on for so long. You know as well as I do that it is the future – the genetic revolution. Think of all the good we have already been able to do – for MS sufferers, Parkinson's, et cetera. And now telomeres. I always respected your decision not to come along on the experiment. It would have been fun the two of us – immortals together! I was sad at first, to do it on my own. I thought it would be lonely. But now I don't mind. I don't feel lonely, after all. I don't mind being a guinea pig – it's much too interesting.' I listened to myself carefully. There was definitely no change in my speaking voice. 'Look at me, I stand before you – the telomere guinea pig!' I screwed up my eyes and sniffed like a pig. 'It's true I feel different. Physically I feel very well, younger than ever. Mentally … well, I suppose you could say, a great burden has lifted. Everything is being turned upside down – it's a kind of spring cleaning.'

MM said, 'But, Victor, you're not immortal, you know.'

I approached him with my hand outstretched. I think I wanted to pat him on the cheek. But he recoiled as if I was an ogre.

I said, 'Don't be afraid, MM. I'm not going to contaminate you. It's true, the genie is out of the bottle. But I'm still human, you know. Actually, more so than ever.'

It was then, I think, that for the first time I had the sensation that I was looking at him through the wrong end of a telescope. Although MM, with his wide Cheshire cat face, was looming over me, he seemed very small. I put out my finger and poked him, in a friendly, teasing way. My finger came to rest in his tummy, which was soft and spongy. He stepped back in alarm, as if my finger was a revolver.

I said, 'MM, you're growing fat!'

I realised that I was able to frighten people. Even the way I said, MM you're growing fat! was a little frightening.

He said, 'Yes. You are exciting phenomenon. But be careful. Soon we will be afraid of you. We want to touch you. Are you real? Soon we begin to think you are alien.'

I laughed. 'Then I will be like you.' MM had once told me that he himself was an alien. 'I can't help it,' I said. 'But I'll never be a real alien like you. I'm only an exciting phenomenon.'

'We are a little afraid of your body.' He leaned forward and fixed me with his globular eyes. 'But we are more afraid of your mind.'

'Who is "we"?' I asked. 'When I walk about in the street nobody points at me. Nobody stares at me in the supermarket. What are you talking about? This experiment is working far better than we expected. Aren't you pleased about that? I would have thought you of all people would be interested in exciting phenomenon. And it is nice, I can tell you, very nice!'

'Yes, it must be a nice feeling ...'

'Have you noticed,' I asked, 'how well things are going here at the lab? I am happy with the way you are all working. I try not to interfere too much, but I know immediately when something is not productive. And I don't mind saying so. Is that what bothers you?'

'No. It's not that ...'

He stared at me across the table.

'What is wrong,' I said, 'with my mind? As far as I am aware my glial cells are in prime condition!'

I began to wonder if he was just a little bit envious. I leaned towards him.

'MM,' I said, softening my voice and trying to put into it all the affection I knew I felt for him. 'Why don't you join me, after all?'

He did an unusual thing: reached out and touched my hand. I felt the pressure of his fingers as if he was examining me. I let him do it for a bit, then withdrew my hand.

'I'm surprised by you, MM,' I said. 'You who are so wild.

Have you lost your sense of adventure? Remember that time when you went into the depths of a park with some mafioso? And had to walk home in your underpants? What about Akira and her nights with the Mongolian chieftain? Not to mention the doorman in Vladivostok with twelve children. Believe me, I don't underestimate your imagination. Without it our telomerase baby might never have seen the light of day. But isn't it rather a waste of that marvellous imagination to have to invent crazy scenarios for yourself? How can a scientist like you believe in such nonsense? Some immaterial soul that metamorphises into one wish-fulfilment after another? Or perhaps you're addicted to these flights of fancy. You don't want the real thing.'

'Imagination,' said MM solemnly, 'is not limited commodity.'

'Oh dear,' I said. 'I know that. My imagination is stronger than ever. But linked to reality.'

MM leaned towards me, and reached for my hand again. 'Victor, my friend …'

I shook my head. 'I'm still the same person, you know. Unlike you I have no alien genes.'

13

Lucy was in London, which was unusual. She preferred Castir, where, she said, she could work better. Although in London too we had a good piano, which needed to be played. But the piano was in the sitting room, and there she easily felt interrupted.

We continued to make love almost as often as before, despite the difficulty of my failing virility. I concentrated hard on Lucy as I had first known her, and tried to recapture the sensations I had once felt. I did not feel the need to summon up images of former lovers, or superimpose other bodies onto hers in my imagination.

But she, I realised, did not do the same.

Once, at the moment of climax, she muttered the word: Alex.

Afterwards, as we lay closely entwined, I asked her: 'Who is Alex?'

'Alex?' she replied. 'I have no idea.'

'But you said his name.'

'Oh no, darling,' she said. 'You imagined that.'

I said nothing.

'It must have been just an exclamation,' she continued, 'of release – whoosh, or something like that.'

I tried it out, teasing her. 'Whoosh! or whalex, or phalex, you mean?'

'You're always imagining things,' she went on. 'Please don't be jealous of nothing – it's so stupid.'

'I'm not jealous.'

How banal, I thought.

'I'm not jealous at all,' I repeated. 'Just curious.'

Then, instead of leaving the matter alone, she persisted: 'Anyway, what would it matter? Even if I had said "Alex". What matters is our happiness now, darling. And you're the one I'm with, you, Victor, my husband.'

This confirmed my suspicions. If there had been nothing to it, she would not have tried to explain. What's more, I knew perfectly well who Alex was, though I pretended not to.

Lucy had once told me, as a kind of foreplay, about her first love.

'He was the nurse,' she had said, 'who looked after my piano teacher, Maya Rosenblum.'

As a teenager she had studied piano with Maya, a distinguished teacher, who had suffered a fall and was in a wheelchair. The male nurse lived in the house with Maya, prepared her meals, and helped her from her chair onto her bed in the evenings.

'Although I loved my lessons,' Lucy had told me, 'I was often thinking about what would happen afterwards. With the nurse. Maya said I was not concentrating properly.'

And afterwards, after the arrival of the next pupil, she would make her way to the kitchen, where the nurse was waiting for her.

'We never made love,' Lucy said. 'Only kissed. I was too young.'

'What was his name?' I asked.

She pretended to try to remember.

'Later,' she said, 'he came to one of my concerts, and wanted to date me seriously. But I was not interested then. He had grown fat, with a double chin, and anyway he was too keen.'

'Too keen?'

'Yes – you know, in those days I was always drawn to difficult situations … until I met you, darling.'

'What was his name?' I asked again.

'Alex,' she replied immediately.

Now, much later, when she muttered 'Alex' as we made love, and then denied it, I was not jealous at all. On the contrary – perhaps it suited me. Was it that it gave me the freedom to be unfaithful myself? I do not think so. With my potency problem, I was not very interested in other women. I could quite happily have done without sex. But Lucy needed it.

She had her eyes closed, but I was sure she hadn't fallen asleep. Nor had I. What I was thinking was this: it will soon be time for my next fix. Telo, I murmured. After all she had exclaimed 'Alex!' Could I not say 'telo'? And I began to laugh to myself. For, I reflected, whatever else, I could not make love to telo. I needed Lucy too.

I pressed against her, reassuringly tight.

My darling Lucy, I thought.

'Are you laughing?' she asked. 'Your body's shaking. Just because you think I said Alex? Does that make you laugh?'

I could tell she was still in love with me; or, perhaps, she was just afraid of being alone.

Lucy was insecure – at least that was what she told me. Personally, I found her strong and confident, but this, she said once, was an illusion. Yet it was strange; to be apparently so sure of herself, and yet, underneath, to tremble, she said, as if she might fall apart. She needed me desperately, it seemed.

And I was quite happy to be her support, her comforting pillow; for I loved her. Whatever else I might feel, I never doubted this; in a profound, almost mystical way, we loved and understood each other. We were 'made' for each other, and, right from the start, we were happy together.

14

The next day I sat with MM in the canteen at the lab. I like to check that the food provided is good and healthy; our scientists need to be properly nourished. The brain is a great consumer of energy.

MM told me about the work he was doing on medication for Parkinson's.

'Working with the genome,' he said, 'is like doing origami. You see what you can make out of it. Is that good English?'

'Very good.'

Then, abruptly, he changed the subject.

'Listen, my friend,' he said, 'let us do it. You agreed.'

'Do what?'

'Publish.'

'Oh that,' I said.

'Why hesitate? We have done experiment – you are experiment. You have patent – nobody can take it from you. But now, little by little, it is time for world to know. It is time to start discussion. Others must decide – not only you – what to do with this. How to proceed.'

As a scientist I knew how important it is, after the initial work has been done, to open the field. I could imagine the fascination our paper would provoke. Our discovery would make the headlines of every newspaper in the world. But beyond this, it was morally right to publish. Such a momentous matter cried out for the attention of the world, for the scrutiny of philosophers and wise men. In the end, whatever the wise men said, people would go mad for telomerase. Who could resist it?

I said in a weak, submissive voice: 'I suppose so. After all, what does it mean, MM? What does it really *mean?*'

'Exactly,' he said. 'That is exactly my point. We cannot know. By ourselves we cannot know. We can only do experiment. It is trauma, Victor. Too much trauma for one person.'

I thought about this. 'I disagree with you, MM. It is not trauma. It is the removal of a trauma. The miseries of old age. General deterioration. At one stroke the main agony of life is gone.'

'Whatever you like,' he said, and shrugged his shoulders.

'Actually,' I said, 'it is all completely normal. The normal progress of medicine.'

I noticed that my left knee was aching slightly; arthritis, I said to myself, to be expected. At my age it was normal to have a spot of arthritis. I rubbed my knee; and it felt different.

Under the table I pulled up the trouser leg. The skin was smooth, and the bone below it, the kneecap, felt smooth too. I was taken by surprise. My knees had, for some years, been growing knobbly; and now, on the left side, the knobbliness was gone. Gone, it seemed, in an instant, from one day to the next, as if planed away in a swift operation; the only sign of change, and this was already diminishing, was a slight ache. Had the whole thing happened while I sat in the canteen? I checked the right knee; it was the same as before, uneven and elderly. But the left was the knee of a boy.

At that moment MM leaned across the table, and took hold of my right arm, at the wrist. He stared into my eyes.

'Please, Victory,' he said. 'The experiment is working. Your mind is sharper than ever. Promise me you will write paper.'

With my left hand, under the table, I continued to rub my knee. It was definitely smooth. This was very exciting; the first clear evidence of bodily improvement.

I toyed with the idea of telling MM; but decided against it.

'Promise you?' I said. 'Why should I promise you anything?'

I felt elated, and laughed.

'Why are you laughing?'

'Because I feel so well. Shouldn't I laugh?'

'Of course. Why not?'

But now he made a serious mistake.

Still gripping my wrist, he leaned towards me and spoke in a low voice, almost a whisper: 'I am sorry, my friend. But the fact is, Victor, if you don't, if you don't publish – I will.' His blue eyes wobbled at me like pregnant jellies. 'My apologies – but I must. It is necessary. It is duty.'

I stared at him. 'Am I hearing you right?' I asked. 'Why so much hostility? I have already told you – I will publish.'

I was still rubbing my knee; and the ache had gone.

But at the same time something quite out of character happened. I have always been patient and tried to understand others. But now icy fury rose up inside me and blood rushed to my head. I pulled away from MM and sat back in the chair. Under the table I touched my knee again – still smooth – and then lowered the trouser leg. MM's face with the jelly eyes came in and out of focus. I had a strong desire to strike it.

'Are you all right, Victory?'

I nodded.

MM stood up and fetched a glass of water from the dispenser. He gave me the water, and I drank it down.

I realised I had to act with caution.

'It's true,' I said, frowning. 'I do go through some funny sensations. I'll write a paper and we'll throw the whole thing open.'

Strategies rushed through my head. Should I sack MM? But if I sacked him nothing could stop him from telling the world. No – I would suppress him. I did not know exactly what to do. But one way or another I would suppress him.

I gave him a big smile, exposing my teeth – my big smile which was so friendly, and which, I was aware, had usually been able to charm people. My smile had often got me out of tricky situations. People had always considered me an honest, generous person. And indeed I was, I thought, as I beamed at MM.

But I was also something else, I realised. I was a master of deception. This was a new thought. Oh, I wouldn't have liked that before, I would have been ashamed to admit it. But now, to my surprise, the realisation filled me with pride. Why pretend, especially to oneself, that one is a modest, humble, self-sacrificing person? Is anyone really like that – if they have the chance to be the opposite? I was becoming a true follower of Nietzsche – that poor, brilliant man who stuck to his beliefs despite so many rejections. And so much loneliness. But did loneliness really matter, after all, if one had brilliance and conviction? As I grimaced at MM I brought my teeth together and executed a few rapid clickety-clacks.

I had a rather amusing thought: my general rejuvenation would not extend to my teeth, which under no circumstances repair themselves. I would be a young man with old teeth. But that was hardly a problem; I would have false teeth and replace them, again and again … and nobody would notice.

I let my smile come gently to rest, and surveyed MM and our little laboratory. I had a moment of intense pleasure. I had every reason to be happy. It was a wild, intoxicating sort of happiness. I was capable of anything and everything. I felt endowed with superhuman strength.

'Thank you,' I said, 'for not telling anyone. You are right to ask me to publish. And I will. I am almost ready – to be a public guinea pig. Then I will publish, and the world will know.'

Once again MM seemed lost for words. One blow from my arm would leave him sprawling on the floor. But instead I terrorised him with my face.

15

It was about a week later that I went out for breakfast. I left Lucy in the apartment, so she could practise without being disturbed. I believe this was what she wanted.

I went to a local café, Le Pain Quotidien, where I had often been before. In this café I always order the same: coffee, soft boiled eggs and a selection of bread. In the old days Victor worried about his cholesterol and asked for just one egg; now I ordered two.

As I sat there, enjoying my breakfast and reading a news-paper, a burly-looking man sat down at the table next to mine. I observed him over the top of my paper; he had a fleshy rectangu-lar face and mousey hair turning grey at the sides. In his forties, I reckoned. He ordered exactly the same as me: two boiled eggs and coffee. It was a coincidence, and we exchanged a glance.

He said, 'This place does good eggs, don't you think?'

I nodded.

The man continued, 'Free range. Everything in this café is organic.'

I was in no mood for small talk, but I said politely, 'Yes. That's why I come here. The prices are a little higher, but it's worth it.'

After a few moments he started again. 'Excuse me for disturb-ing you. You'd probably like to be left alone.'

'Not at all.'

'The thing is,' the man went on, 'I recognise you. We did an article about you in the *Guardian*. I am the science correspondent.'

'Yes, I remember.'

'We had a photo of you too. You developed a drug to help MS sufferers.'

'My laboratory did.'

'We thought you would get a Nobel for that.'

I smiled. 'Not yet, anyway,' I said. 'It's not a cure.'

'All the same, you're a hero. How many people have been helped by your work.'

'Thank you.'

The waitress came to our table. 'Something else?' she inquired.

'May I offer you another coffee?' the man asked me. 'It's a privilege to meet you in the flesh.'

I sighed. 'Thank you,' I said.

'This is a lucky break for me,' he continued. 'Do you mind if I pick your brains a tiny bit?'

'If I can be of any help.'

'The thing is,' the man said, 'I'm researching an article on the imagination – imaginative sympathy, to be precise. As I'm sure you know, there's a lot of interest at the moment about altruism, where does the altruistic impulse come from, and so on.'

'An important subject.'

'Yes – I'm sure I don't have to tell you about mirror neurons. Do you think mirror neurons play a part in altruism?'

At the mention of mirror neurons I became suspicious. I immediately thought of MM, who is obsessed by them; what had he been up to behind my back? Journalists will do anything to trick people into giving away their secrets. For them a saleable story is all that matters. In all likelihood this man had been tracking me.

'Yes,' I said. 'I believe that mirror neurons enable us to feel sympathy for others. And imagination, that limitless faculty, does the rest.'

'Do you think,' he continued, 'that the mirror neurons in our brains function from the very start of life? Or do they have to be stimulated into action?'

'Like all brain cells,' I replied, 'they have to be exercised. Even the cleverest people use only a proportion of their brain potential.'

'Of course. And so the same must go for mirror neurons. Can they also atrophy, in some circumstances?'

'All brain cells are subject to disease.'

'Yes, but in a healthy individual?'

'Probably.'

I had a strong desire to say to the man: Get to the point! But I held back.

'I can see you know a lot about them,' I said.

Flattery, in my experience, usually works.

'Naturally I have been doing my research. But you are the person I have wanted to contact. This is a most extraordinary coincidence ...'

I raised my eyebrows. I do not believe in coincidence, especially where journalists are concerned. The man smiled; he realised that I could not be so easily duped.

'All right,' he said. 'I will tell you the truth. The fact is, we have been contacted by a scientist from your laboratory. A Russian gentleman.'

'Really?'

'Yes, Mr Makarevich.'

'One of our best researchers. He is a great talker. I am sure he was helpful.'

'He assured me that you would be happy to talk to the *Guardian* – a newspaper which, as you know, has always been most favourably inclined to your work.'

'Unfortunately,' I said, 'Mr Makarevich is not entirely reliable. His imagination, you see, knows no bounds. And this sometimes leads him into the domain of fantasy.'

'We had a most interesting talk. I met up with him personally.' Now I saw it coming. 'He mentioned, among other things, that you yourself are conducting an experiment into the ageing process. He said that you are about to publish your results in the *Lancet*. Could you tell me a little about it?'

The journalist looked at me with eager, innocent eyes. It was all so obvious, I thought. The man would not have made a good interrogator.

'With pleasure,' I said. 'But we are at a very elementary stage.'

'Mr Makarevich told me about telomerase.'

'Yes, an interesting enzyme.'

'He gave me the impression that you yourself are trying out an anti-ageing drug.'

I thought about this. Why should I not talk to a newspaper? But I said, 'Oh dear. It's just wishful thinking, I'm afraid.'

'Mr Makarevich was quite clear.'

'I will be frank with you, Mr ...?'

'Robinson.'

'I will be frank with you, Mr Robinson. Especially as you come from the *Guardian*. It is true that we are researching various compounds relating to telomerase. We are interested in developing a drug that has the potential to stimulate the production of telomerase within our cells. But it is dangerous, you see. Because in cancer cells the enzyme telomerase is active. The fact is, that the implementation of an anti-ageing drug based on telomerase would inevitably lead to cancer.'

'Yes, Mr Makarevich mentioned the possibility of cancer. But he said that you were trying out the new drug anyway – on yourself. And I wondered how you were getting on.'

'It will be a long time,' I said, 'before we can deal effectively with the problem of ageing. There are no short cuts. Now, without being rude, I think I have told you enough. The details of this matter are complex. When we discover anything of importance, I will publish the results in an appropriate paper.'

'Thank you,' said Mr Robinson. 'I will not trouble you further.'

With that I took up my newspaper again. But the thought of MM giving away our secret enraged me.

So I continued, in a low voice: 'Poor Mr Makarevich. What you tell me about his state of mind worries me considerably.' I was quite sure the journalist was listening, though he pretended to be concentrating on his breakfast. Probably, I thought, he was also recording my words.

'You see,' I went on, 'Mr Makarevich is a great inventor of stories. For example, he believes in reincarnation. Did he tell you about his past lives? Mr Makarevich, I am afraid, will make up anything to suit himself.'

'Yes,' said the man. 'I myself had the impression that he was a little unstable. However, if I may ask, have you nevertheless submitted a patent for the anti-ageing research?'

This question vexed me; it was none of his business. But I realised it might be a good way of putting an end to the conversation.

'I'm glad you asked this,' I replied. 'Yes indeed. We submitted a patent, as usual, at the start of the research.' I paused. Then continued, 'Our research is about telomerase in general. As I explained to you, in cancer cells the gene for telomerase is switched on. This opens up various possibilities for the treatment of cancer. Any discovery relating to the ageing process would be merely a by-product.'

'That is good news,' said Mr Robinson. 'Knowing your reputation I expect you will come up with something significant. Cancer may soon become a disease of the past. And of course you, of all people, know how important it is to patent research at an early stage.'

'I do indeed. And I can tell you, in confidence, that a certain amount of venture capital has already come our way.'

This was true; the extra money was a great help in funding the production of telo. I was pleased with the way I had diverted the man's attention to cancer.

I began to have an unusual sensation; an odd pressure was building up inside me, and heat was rising through my body. And there was, for a moment, a rumbling inside my head, a grating sound like the shifting of gravel. I was afraid my face and neck were becoming red. It was a nasty moment. Was I about to have a stroke?

But this sensation passed quickly, and I returned to normal. A burst of energy buzzed through my body, and I looked at Mr Robinson with cool calm eyes.

I saw him all too clearly.

Small black forests blossomed in the man's ears, and his heavy rectangular face looked lopsided. His eyebrows were bushy, and a few straggling hairs curled away from the rest.

I summoned all my power and directed it into the man's face. Mouthing the words silently, I commanded: heart attack.

At the same time I continued in a quiet voice: 'Perhaps I shouldn't say this to you, but Mr Makarevich is excessively concerned with money. Funding, Victor, funding! he says to me. His continued employment is, understandably, a matter of great importance to him. Not to mention his own glory. I am sure you have come across this type of researcher before. No, I shouldn't say that. Mr Makarevich is a good scientist, but sometimes he takes his dreams for reality. He can't always tell the difference.' I was being unfair, yet there was some truth in what I said.

I went on: 'Mr Makarevich has been involved with our telomerase research from the beginning. Not content with the possibility of treating cancer, he has imagined that we are also producing an anti-ageing drug. And so he has persuaded himself, it seems, that such a drug actually exists, and that I myself am the first guinea pig! But nothing could be further from the truth. You have been a victim, I am afraid, Mr Robinson, of his excessive imagination. If he really believed we had invented such a drug, why didn't he try it on himself? Because he knows, of course, deep down, that this is a fantasy. And I have to say, reluctantly, that he would probably be far too cowardly to take such a step himself.'

I stood up and went to pay for my breakfast. I noticed, as I picked up the bill from my table, that my left thumb seemed slightly longer than usual, almost as long as the other fingers. But this was probably an illusion; it was the way I was holding the paper.

'Goodbye, Mr Robinson,' I said. 'It's been a pleasure talking to you. If you have any questions about mirror neurons, please do not hesitate to contact me.'

I gave him my professional email address.

16

Journalists! I have always been in favour of a free, investigative press. But now I was beginning to have my doubts. Journalists are trained to be intrusive; this can be most annoying.

I decided to go for a holiday.

Lucy was away on a concert tour in Germany, a country she often visited. She had a series of performances there with Niko, her duo partner, a cellist.

So where would I go? I considered making a long journey, to an exotic location. After all, I could be away for two weeks and be back in time to take the medication. Lucy would not miss me. And the lab in Archway could function without my presence.

But another, closer destination pulled at me: Rome. The eternal city, where I had always felt happy and free, and where I had had my first insights into the mechanism of age. It was a long time since I had been to Rome, so why not?

With some excitement I took the train from Paris, the Palatino, which leaves in the evening and arrives in Rome the next morning.

As a young man Victor loved this journey. He liked sleeping on the train. I took a couchette, as before.

Perhaps, I thought, an old couple would share my compartment. I was becoming quite interested in the old – they were touching; so slow at everything. I think it was my sense of history; the old were remnants of another age. I saw them as unfortunate victims, born too soon; they could do nothing about it.

But, as it happened, my only companion was a boy, sixteen or seventeen years old.

This boy was going to Chambéry, to a conference of students. And there, he told me, he would be representing his school. His subject was science; he intended to be a biologist. He was fair and tall and in his clear eyes was both intelligence and idealism.

We talked. I said that never has there been a more exciting time to be a biologist. I told him about our laboratory; about stem cell research and the successes and failures we have had in this field. I explained about auto-immune disorders, and the progress we were making on lupus, arthritis and MS.

The boy's name was Luc. Luke was the name we nearly gave to our baby. We decided against Luke because it was too much like Lucy.

Then something happened. My heart began to beat unusually fast. I could feel it pounding, and sat down on the edge of the lower bunk.

I said, 'Shall I let you into a secret?'

He nodded enthusiastically.

'After all you're a biologist too.'

Was I about to tell a complete stranger?

Better not, I thought. I could easily tell him about something else.

And yet, suddenly, I couldn't stop myself.

'Remember telomeres?' I said.

Luc was not sure.

I opened my mouth, and out it came. Well, why not? He was only a boy. A hot flush rose through my face to the roots of my hair.

Unable to control my excitement I said, 'We have found a way of repairing telomeres. And what is the result?'

The boy shrugged. 'Tell me,' he said.

'The chromosomes tighten. And the ageing process is halted.'

'Really?'

'There is nothing inevitable about ageing,' I went on. 'Telomerase repairs telomeres. If the supply of telomerase is maintained, we do not have to grow old. Ageing is a malfunction. It can be treated.'

The boy was listening carefully. He frowned and said nothing.

I continued, 'Maintaining the correct supply of telomerase is a subtle process. It has to do with controlling the balance of the cellular environment. Discovering how to do this precisely is our achievement.'

I paused. A new thought niggled at me. Was it possible that someone else, in some other lab, had made the same discovery?

But this was paranoia. I knew perfectly well that we had taken out a patent on our research. The patent was vaguely worded, but had been accepted. In the submission we had explained something of our work on telomerase, in general. We were protected.

I said, 'As a matter of fact the therapy works even better than we expected. It is possible not only to halt the ageing process – but actively to rejuvenate. That is, if you start the treatment in middle age, for example, and you dose it carefully, the telomeres actually lengthen. The chromosomes tighten and become more efficient, as in youth. And the patient grows younger.' Now I spoke quietly, soberly. 'It's logical, if you think about it.'

After a moment Luc said, 'But have you tried this out? On a real person? Or are these just lab results?'

I replied, 'Yes, we have tried it out. We are trying it out. On a real person. We have one guinea pig. And the results are better than expected.'

'Only one person?'

'Yes. There were supposed to be two more. But they called it off at the last moment. They were afraid, you see.'

I could hardly believe I was disclosing all this. As if a machine had been set in motion, and I had no power over it.

The boy was silent. He was trying to digest it. He repeated, 'Only one person ... one person in the whole world?'

I nodded. And suddenly the boy smiled.

I stood up; and almost embraced him. My chest and my armpits were sweaty. I could feel my shirt sticking to my body.

I said, 'Don't tell anyone.'

'I won't,' he replied.

'Just between us.'

I took a deep breath.

I said, 'Old age is a sad thing. Perhaps you're too young to understand. But you will, one day. Nobody would want to live for ever with all the infirmities of old age. But that is the beauty of our treatment. You have experience and wisdom – and yet you are young. It's the oldest dream of mankind.'

Luc lowered his eyes. It was a lot to take in. He stepped back and leaned against the door of the compartment.

I said, 'You're still a boy. But as you grow older the idea of ageing and dying becomes more and more absurd. To be old and decrepit when you don't *feel* old and decrepit. It just seems like a stupid mistake.'

'Unless you feel you've had enough,' he said unexpectedly.

'Ah yes. You might feel that. With all the stiffness, the exhaustion, the aches, the small strokes often unnoticed … So far the disease of ageing and decline has been incurable; but, as you know, to a medical researcher "incurable" only means – incurable at the moment. And now it's another moment.'

Luc said nothing.

I went on: 'All this sounds strange to you. But one day it will be normal – as normal as antibiotics. Everybody will want it – you too.'

I waited for him to say something, or at least to smile again. In the old days people smiled at me easily. Sometimes, in the street, even strangers smiled at me as they passed. But Luc didn't smile now. He watched me warily.

I laughed and said, 'You needn't be suspicious or frightened of me. I'm just the same as everybody else. Better, in fact.'

Yet even as I spoke, I wondered. How pathetic to say: I'm just the same as everybody else. In fact I wasn't like anybody else at all.

I brushed past Luc and went into the corridor. 'I'm going to the restaurant,' I said. 'Would you like to come? I'll invite you.'

'Thank you very much but I've had dinner.'

I turned back to him. I was elated. 'You see, there's nothing inevitable about ageing. After a certain age the genes lose interest. That's all. As long as they're passed to the next generation they have no interest in keeping a body alive and well. That's what it's all about. That's what I mean when I say that ageing is a malfunction. Now, for the first time, we'll be able to treat it. It's no monstrous intervention, you know. We're all subject to the laws of chemistry. The gene for telomerase is present naturally in all our cells. We just give it a little tweak. Sure you won't come to the restaurant?'

'No, thank you very much.'

'Our destiny is chemical, you see. Like everything else. Biological processes are all chemical, in essence. That's exactly what's so fascinating about being a biologist. Everything is quite clearly material. Alter the chemistry slightly and you can cause a revolution. What time do you get to Chambéry?'

'Three o'clock.'

'Well, good night. Get some sleep.'

◆◆

I made my way to the dining car. As I moved through the train I felt the presence of my baby son.

He was there – in the glass of the windows, in the black night, the long corridor, in the jolting spaces between carriages. I stopped, pressed my forehead against the cool glass. I spoke to him: My baby ... I have never loved you more than I do now, I have never felt closer to you ...

I came back from the restaurant and found my bright schoolboy asleep on the top bunk. He had kindly switched on the little reading light above my own berth. It was eleven o'clock. His breathing was regular. On the floor were his shoes, a pair of large white trainers neatly stacked under the bunk. I picked up the shoes and smelt the odour of a teenager. I put my fingers right inside and felt the sweaty softness of the soles. I stepped out into the corridor and closed the door carefully.

Now I am not sure how this happened. But as I made my way down the corridor, going nowhere in particular, I was carrying his shoes. I stopped in the concertina gap between carriages. It was a noisy place, unstable as in the trains of my youth. I leaned against the shifting panels and closed my eyes. My fingers were jammed inside the canvas trainers.

Somebody was approaching. I crossed into the next carriage and went into the toilet. I saw my face in the mirror: black eyebrows and fleshy lips. The hair on my head was glossy and thick. The upper lip looked dark, as if brushed by tar.

The universal wolf, I said laughing silently, and watched my mouth move.

Then I put the shoes down, in the corner between the toilet and washbasin. I left them there.

At a quarter to three I called to Luc in the upper bunk. He woke with a start and immediately the little staccato alarm went off on his wristwatch. Out of consideration for me he did not put on the light. He climbed down the ladder and began dressing, his quick hands finding shirt and trousers exactly where he had left them. Then I heard him reaching under the bunk, pausing as if to recollect, then searching again. Dimly I saw him bending down, heard his hands sweeping the floor. To help him I switched on my reading light. It was nearly five to three. I roused myself and asked him what was the matter. He told me. Lost his shoes? We agreed that this was a very unlikely occurrence. I suggested that he might have left them outside the door. An absurd idea, but I went into the corridor to check. In my socks. It was very cold.

Now I have a thing about shoes, I'm not sure why. Out in

the wild I sometimes take them off and go barefoot. Once a colleague gave me a piece of the oldest shoe ever found. In a cave in Armenia.

I think I had been intending to present the schoolboy with his trainers at the last moment, like a 'deus ex machina'. I set off down the corridor, aware that I must hurry. But the train was already slowing down. My pace slackened and I returned to the compartment empty-handed. I don't know why I was tormenting Luc in this way. 'Oh we'll find them,' I said. On my hands and knees I peered under the bunks, while with swift awkward movements Luc hauled himself to the upper levels, then leapt down.

The train stopped. I looked out. The platform was covered in snow and ice; though winter was long over. Chambéry is high in the mountains.

The poor resourceful schoolboy was at his wits' end. I thought of dashing down the train to the toilet, but there was no time. Besides it would have looked rather odd.

'You must wait in the station hall,' I said. 'And in the morning go and buy yourself some new ones.'

I gave him a pair of thick brown socks from my own luggage. 'But I haven't got enough money ...'

From my pocket I took two hundred euros. Luc dragged his rucksack to the door; then quickly took out a pen and asked for my address. I saw beads of sweat glueing his blond curls to his forehead. He was almost in tears. He turned and stepped onto the frozen platform in my socks. He heaved his rucksack onto his back and, as the cold reached him, hopped from one foot to the other. I watched him skipping along, as if on burning coals, and then running. The pack lurched to and fro against his back. He reached the door of the waiting room, but it was, I could just see, locked.

The train left.

Later I went back to the toilet. A pool of dirty water was rolling across the floor, and one of the trainers was wet and stained. I picked them up and left them on the ledge by the little window.

I cannot commend this boy too highly. When I returned to Castir there was a small package waiting for me, with my socks, the money and a postcard of the mountains.

◆◆

In my hotel in Rome I reproached myself severely. What a thing to do – it was completely out of character.

While unpacking I saw my hands. On the right, the skin was loose and marked with brown spots, as it had been for some years; but the left hand was clear and unwrinkled. This was a pleasant surprise; yet, in a way, I was expecting it. I checked my knees. They had not changed; the left smooth, the right still knobbly.

It was fortunate, I smiled to myself, that I couldn't see my inner organs: one kidney young, the other old; the liver soft and spongy, the pancreas brittle and dry. But the medication was working, in its own way. My body was indeed repairing itself – though unevenly.

I went quite cheerfully out into the city. In Piazza Navona I gazed at the fountain sculpted by Bernini, and decorated with gods – the gods that represented the four great rivers of the world. Gods could be invented for anything, and the Romans did it. That was a good idea. A joyful way to move through life, accompanied at every step by divinities. Buoyed up by illusion; what else could people do?

In the Campidoglio I stood above the Roman Forum. Ruined temples, shrines and triumphal arches lay spread out before me. It was the utter stillness of this place that had always appealed to me. Trees and bushes sprouted from stray seeds and had turned the Forum into a garden.

I leaned on an iron railing and surveyed the scene.

Then I went to see the chapel in the French church, painted by Caravaggio.

It was darker than I remembered. Old Victor had loved these paintings intensely. They filled him with the 'great emotions' he was so partial to.

In the first, Jesus enters in a dusty beam and with a raised, curved finger summons Matthew, the tax collector, who sits with his companions at a table, counting money.

In the next picture an illiterate barefoot Matthew writes the Gospel, his pen guided by a playful angel.

In the last, Matthew, old and careworn, is slain by a glowing youth.

It was as I remembered: everything captured there, the spirit and the flesh, light and dark, fixed for ever. An immortal vision.

I focused on Christ's finger, pointing at Matthew, in the first picture. Time to look up, I whispered to Matthew, who sat unaware, head bowed over his pile of money, fingers splayed on the table. Ridiculous as it was I found myself becoming annoyed with this grubby adolescent. Go on, I told him, look up! I wanted the next instalment. Now I spoke to Christ's finger. Move! I said. After a period of intense concentration it seemed to me that the finger had in fact moved a centimetre or two. I stared so hard that my eyes began to water.

Suddenly a cackle escaped me. I couldn't help it; the reverent silence around me was funny. A respectable old couple were taken by surprise and shot me an angry look as if I was a hooligan. I smiled apologetically. Then, as they turned back to the pictures, I let loose another louder cackle which echoed round the chapel.

Without waiting for the reaction of the old couple I set off to inspect the rest of the church. It was fairly ordinary. A limping priest in a black skirt locked himself into a confessional. Immediately a small round woman with a moustache rose from a pew and took her place on the other side of that box of darkness. A few other crab-like creatures were dotted about the pews, waiting for death.

Enormously tall I glided across the marble floors and returned for a last glimpse of the Caravaggios.

The ancient couple who had so disapproved of me were leaving the side chapel. They could hardly walk and leaned on sticks. I positioned myself in front of them and prepared for their angry faces.

The old man's skin was so bunched and pleated that at first I could hardly locate his eyes. Then I saw that they were almost closed, but wet, and an oblong tear was rolling down each cheek.

For a moment I wondered if this was because of my loutish manners. I was hardly behaving like an awestruck tourist. But then I realised it was the pictures. He was weeping for Caravaggio!

I stared at him. He seemed himself to be a picture, an antique work preserved on the wall of a mildewed chapel, a warning for future generations, a 'memento mori'.

He walked vaguely, as though blind. Beside him his wife moved with difficulty, very quietly, her feeble eyes wide, glimmering like distant stars. Her hand, resting on his, was so worn it was already a skeleton. I saw quite clearly her pale disintegrating bones.

But suddenly this living tableau struck me as appallingly beautiful. Yet it was everything that I was trying never to be.

Unwilling to lose them I pursued as they made their way like snails, often pausing for rest, through the streets of Rome. Effervescent, hard as a diamond, gleaming with telomerase, I towered over them, so close I could have touched them. Thickets of white hair sprouted from the old man's ears; below his bald pate on the back of his neck was a rubbery growth. With my X-ray eyes I undressed him, an awful compilation of gristle, blotch and flab.

But his face, as I had seen it after Caravaggio, was filled with something that hit me like a bullet: infinite tenderness. Tenderness! Suddenly the face of this old wreck appeared to me the most beautiful thing in the world. As if consumed with sorrow I cried out for this balm, reached out for it, tried to draw it greedily into myself; then my own implacable face seemed to dissolve, my iron flesh, as if a healing hand passed across my eyes.

I lost my old couple in the Jewish quarter, where they went into a restaurant beside Teatro Marcello.

And now I went through Rome drenched with feeling. As if a dam had burst and a reservoir had broken its bounds. But what type of 'feeling' was this? Almost everybody I saw, but especially the hunched, the crippled, the wretched, caused obscure pangs of recognition. I saw myself in every withered limb, every shred of skin. At random I pursued one or another, matching their poor step, I could hardly hold back from hugging them; instead like a missile I directed myself against their decomposing backs; plunging inside I was cradled, eyes shut, ears stopped, by nerves, tendons, cartilage, soft slippery shapes; yes, I forced myself inside them, breath for breath, heart for heart, panting with thirst, longing, need, as if begging for some kind of odd shameful union.

This extraordinary sensation, this terrible, unexpected desire for the old, was beyond my control; agonising though it was, it seemed as if my life depended on it, soft, horrible, yet I couldn't stop myself ...

Then I tripped against something, and came to my senses.

Where was I? Looming above me was the dark figure of Giordano Bruno. On a plinth, carved in black, were scenes of his trial by the Inquisition, and public burning. Against these carvings I pressed my fingers and palms. Giordano Bruno: condemned to death for freedom of thought.

I tried to climb up onto the plinth but it was slippery and I kept falling back. Then somebody pulled me down. A small crowd had gathered, obviously taking me for a madman. People can't resist a lunatic. I could have got down on hands and knees and howled like a dog ... but then I was no sort of lunatic they could understand.

So I cut through the crowd – and the next thing I noticed was children.

◆◆

It was four o'clock and Rome was full of them. They were tugging at their mothers' sleeves, playing ball against the walls of ancient churches, walking home from school with satchels on their backs. Their twittering filled the air. Sunlight glowed on the bricks and stone.

One little girl particularly took my fancy. From her skinny shoulder hung a bright red bag, where a crouching Spiderman stood out in relief. I bounced along behind, watching the bag as it tap-tapped against her back. She was about ten years old, I reckoned. A sullen woman in a long skirt, perhaps a nanny, walked beside her. We crossed the Jewish quarter, Piazza Mattei with the Tortoise fountain, up the steps to Campidoglio, down beside the Forum.

I named my young companion: Felicity.

Images poured through my head. I saw myself, Victor, the little sensitive boy, munching a biscuit with his mother in Kenwood. His eyes slant downwards; he is trying to look like the photograph of Andres. His springy curls are just like Felicity's.

Ahead rose the Palatine Hill; there among the ruins a host of magnificent maladjusted emperors processed before my inner eye.

Palatino! I replayed Luc and the train, the serious responsible schoolboy as he hops in his socks along the icy platform. I saw him as he tiptoes to the waiting room and finds it locked. Embarrassed, his feet freezing by the second, he pleads with the stationmaster. But probably, at this hour, there is no stationmaster. There is only the guard, who will hurry back to bed as soon as the Palatino has passed through. The boy looks back at the train; the guard slams the metal door, I stand on the inside step, the train begins to move. Good luck, Luc! I say aloud, feeling quite together with him in the odd painful adventure I have contrived; the wheels creak as if breaking ice, I press my cheek against the glass.

Did I do this?

Now amid the tourists we passed the Colosseum, where

Christians were thrown to the lions for the enjoyment of specta-
tors, and I seemed to be gaining on Felicity – I mean it was as if
I could no longer keep a sensible distance – already I seemed to
be pressing, under the red satchel, between her shoulder blades
– then battering my way into her, languishing inside, bathing in
her tight little body, her pristine inner space, utterly untouched
by death … yet there she was, meanwhile, bobbing ahead of me
unawares with her Spiderman bag and grim companion, and
now skipping up the cobbled hill beside the Church of St John
and Paul, and in through the gates of Villa Celimontana.

I took hold of the iron gatepost and stopped, my breath
rather fast. The metal was cool.

I regained my composure.

Felicity entered the shady, rolling park, sat down on a bench
and opened her bag. Meanwhile the nanny set off on her own; I
could see she was going to the lavatory, an ugly building hidden
in laurel bushes. From her bag Felicity took a piece of chocolate
cake and a bottle of lemonade. She began to eat with the utmost
delicacy, carefully retrieving each crumb that fell on her blouse
and cleaning her lips with her tongue after each mouthful. I
stood in front of her and she looked at me. She looked at me
with interest and smiled. I think she nearly gave me a piece of
her chocolate cake.

She was the most perfect child I had ever seen.

She had certainly been told not to speak to strangers. Yet she
was, I could see, naturally communicative. She wanted to say
something, or at least offer me a piece of chocolate cake. But
it was teatime after school and she was hungry. She finished
the cake and opened the bag again. This time I am sure she
was looking for something for me. But I could see the nanny
approaching, almost running, across the grass.

I held out my right hand; it was blotchy, and I withdrew it
quickly.

'Goodbye,' I said. 'Do you speak English?'

Felicity laughed. 'Yes,' she said, 'I speak.'

'You speak English? Where did you learn?'

She replied, 'I have an English grandmother.'

I was so pleased to hear her voice.

I said, 'I think I shall give up my drug and become human again.'

But this of course she did not understand. She lifted up her hands helplessly and laughed again. The nanny glared at me, zipped up the Spiderman bag, and led her away.

I watched them leave the park by the same gate, hoping that Felicity might turn and look at me again; but she did not.

◆◆

At first I felt rather alone, but not for long. There were other children in the park, dashing to and fro on scooters and skateboards; but I was not drawn to them.

I recovered. For a time I had burst through my skin like a hernia, but now I popped back and was sealed again as before.

The park filled up with people of all ages, men, women, couples, families with pushchairs, grandparents. I wandered in the evening sunlight among all these humans, leading lives of quiet despair (as Freud said); and heads of the dead, on plinths. There was not much difference between the two – the living would so soon be dead.

Unless I saved them.

At the far end of the park a staircase entwined with wisteria led down to a lower level. There was a kind of grotto, very dark and dirty, with little stalactites irregularly dripping water. At the back of the cave I could just make out a stone figure covered in weeds and moss. In fading light the statues that grace Roman parks can sometimes be mistaken for the living. But this one was much larger than life.

My eyes soon adjusted to the dim light.

A huge naked male on hands and knees was perching on a steep piece of rock. His hair was thick and matted and fell to the ground. His face was turned towards me, melancholy, furrowed, the eyes bulbous, the skin discoloured and pitted with holes. One ankle dragged behind it a segment of chain. At the base of the statue was an inscription, entirely obscured by moss.

I scraped at the moss and eventually made out these letters: PROM-TE- LI—RATO. Four letters were illegible. But you did not have to be a great linguist to guess what they were.

PROMETEO. LIBERATO.

PROMETHEUS UNBOUND

The massive figure stared blindly towards me. Yet he was smiling. The upper lip was almost entirely worn away, but the lower was full and curved.

My knowledge of Prometheus was sketchy. But I knew this: Prometheus stole the secret of fire from the gods and gave it to man. He was a benefactor. With the secret of fire, man could challenge the gods and be their equal. For this crime the immortals chained him to a rock for ever. And now, against the will of the gods, his chains had been severed.

Prometheus smiled and I smiled back. Who had set him free? I did not know. But he had broken his chains. He was on all fours – but, after all, he hadn't walked for a long time. He had to get used to it. I remembered this too: the gods sent an eagle each day to consume his liver. But each night it grew again because Prometheus was immortal.

A large wooden stick lay in the grotto beside him. Had someone left it there on purpose – as if to help him stand up?

♦♦

I left the Villa Celimontana with a buoyant step. The encounter with Prometheus had restored my good humour.

A rosy sunset enveloped the Eternal City. Outside the park gates I passed the basilica of Saints Giovanni and Paolo, and decided to pay a visit, as to an old friend.

In I went, just as the door was closing. The caretaker looked at me crossly, but I took a fifty-euro note from my wallet, and gave it to him. From this church, I knew, a staircase led down to an ancient Roman street. This was where I wanted to go. The caretaker took me to the back of the church and unlocked a door in the wall; there before me was the dusty staircase lit by a single bulb. I assured him I wouldn't be long.

Down, down I went, enjoying every step. It was almost as if, once again, I was there with you. With you, Victor of old. And with L.

With each step a century was reborn. At the bottom was the ancient Roman street in an excellent state of preservation. The houses lay open, their mosaics and murals almost intact.

Do you remember, Lucy? It was dark. We took off our shoes and socks. Were we the first people in two thousand years to walk barefoot on those cold floors?

I did it again. Then, in the last house I sat cross-legged on the ground before an antique wall painting: a naked young woman in a boat, her back turned. Her flesh is soft and white. She is crossing the river Styx to the land of the Dead. But her face and sad eyes look back at us, the living.

We saw her together, do you remember? We said, laughing, that she had a look of you. Her eyes, dark like yours, are resigned. Though in your eyes, Lucy, I have never seen resignation. Yours are shy and wild. This dead woman is soft, she has none of your fire. She is plump and sensual. There is no resemblance, except perhaps in the shape of the chin. Was that what we meant? We laughed and then we kissed. We found it erotic. We found almost everything erotic.

I still understand the word erotic. And there, alone in the ancient street I felt it again – in the soles of my feet as I walked barefoot in that place. Erotic. Of course I expected, as I grew younger, to be gloriously erotic.

But love is loneliness, you see. Lack. Fear of death. I wonder what else it is. It must be something more than that. It is sharing, of course, sharing. We gasp for love. Victor gasped for love. Religions are made of that, religions, art and music. We don't realise, at the time, what we create – from lack.

I looked with indifference at that poor young woman on the wall sailing seductively to her death. I admired the skill of the ancient artist and was touched that she was still there, just as naked after so many centuries. But my indifference was phenomenal. Indifferent as nature itself.

I don't think I had ever realised it so clearly: that everything we are supposed to prize most highly comes only from lack. A series of heroic, heart-rending palliatives. Like me, as I rammed my way into the bodies of the grotesque old people, and then Felicity. It was funny. I couldn't help finding that funny, it seemed already far away, even the tears I almost shed watching the perfect child eating her chocolate cake on the bench were funny now. I do have a sense of humour. If one day everybody starts doing telo, as they will, let's hope they don't lose that – humour.

The caretaker came downstairs with a torch and glared at me. He shone the torch rudely in my eyes. He even put out his hand as if to say I'd been there far too long and he required another fifty euros. But this was unreasonable. I had no desire to stay any longer.

I thanked the caretaker politely, and made my way back up the stairs to the land of the others; and decided to have dinner in the lovely restaurant beside the Teatro Marcello, in the Jewish quarter, where I had earlier lost my old couple.

I sat on the terrace outside, and basked in the glory of Rome on a warm evening. The Teatro Marcello now had a fence around it; it would have been difficult to creep through and sit among the ancient columns, as I had once done as a young man.

17

In the evenings, after dinner, I sometimes walked along the banks of the river Tiber. Right in the centre of the city these low embankments were wild and untended. The din of traffic and people was dulled by high walls. There were rats, rubbish, a few stray dogs, occasional lovers. Here and there groups of youths huddled under bridges. Huge plane trees grew amid rough grass and pressed their branches into the streets above. Light seeped down through the leaves, from tall, dim lamps.

I sat for a while on a stone bench, and let my mind go blank. A vapour hung over the water; how beautiful, I said to myself. How mysterious. Rome. Rome! In the old days, perhaps, I would have been overcome by emotion, a touching sense of nostalgia would have pressed like a clammy hand against my throat. I said it aloud: like a clammy hand against my throat. I smiled. The face of Prometheus, the benefactor, his blind stare and lipless grin, came back to me. I too had a gift for mankind. Years had passed since I began taking telo, I am not sure how many. But now at last I knew what had to be done; I could not understand why I had delayed so long. I had to publish, open the debate, discuss. The time had come.

It was a relief to make this decision. I stood up, as if to go back to the hotel and start writing an article straightaway. I said aloud: Yes, it is time to share.

I took a few firm steps along the river bank. Not far away, on the next bench, an old man was sitting with a bottle of wine. The sight of this tramp disturbed me. We all know how easy it is, when decisions lie on a knife edge, to go another way. Perhaps it was the smell of urine that assaulted me as I approached.

I said quietly: You are a human being like me.

Yet at the same time I was tempted to fling him bodily into the river. I had a moment of indecision, then I found myself nodding politely at the poor decrepit creature. I waited for a reaction, but there was none. As if leaving it to my legs, I turned and wandered back to the stone seat. Then, quite automatically, without thinking, I took off my coat; folded it and laid it on the bench, a fine camel hair overcoat I had bought a few days before. Concealed in an inside pocket was 300 euros.

I still had the stick with me, the solid wooden stick I had picked up in the Villa Celimontana. It had been lying beside Prometheus. The giant had been eyeing it as if it might help him start walking upright again. Which was quite difficult after so many centuries chained to the rock. But I took the stick because poor old P. carved in stone would never be able to reach out and grab it – and now I put it on the ground under the bench. I moved away from the bench where my overcoat lay and looked across the river. Old Father Tiber, I thought; what have you seen!

The misty vapour still hung over the water. I waited. Sooner than expected I heard, with my sharp ears, steps behind me. Then I smelt him. As though watching through the back of my head I knew exactly what was happening. I gave him time. Then I turned and made a run for the bench. The old fellow was so engrossed, passing his hands all over the silky coat and searching in the pockets, that I reached the bench and picked up the cudgel before he saw me. Then, as I brandished the cudgel in his face, he stumbled backwards and fell over. I raised the stick as if to strike him with all my strength. He made his getaway on all fours, then hobbled to his feet and ran as fast as he could, dragging one leg. The wine bottle slipped from his grasp and crashed onto the stones.

I re-arranged my coat, folded it neatly on the bench and returned to the water's edge, taking the cudgel with me.

In my head I began to prepare the article I would write for *Genome*. I had to decide how much to relate. I would not describe my own experience but state the scientific facts. These would not come as a surprise to many researchers. Telomerase has been talked about for a long time. But it has not been in the news much recently, because of the link with cancer. This has frightened people off. So now they look helplessly for other ways of curing old age.

From the corner of my eye, as I stood by the water, I saw a new person approaching on the bank. A youngish man in a denim jacket was wandering along rather aimlessly, his head dangling to one side. He went straight past the bench, then stopped and came back. He bent down and inspected the coat. I thought I might let him have it. There was something pleasant about him. He was rather like me in shape and size, his hair curly, though fair. He lifted up the coat and tried it on. It was a good fit, even over the denim jacket.

I thought I might let him get away with it. Nevertheless I began to walk towards him, slowly, very quietly. He didn't notice until I was right up behind him. Then he got a shock, rapidly took off the coat and muttered apologies. He walked away fast, half turning and making conciliatory gestures. Once again I arranged the coat neatly on the bench. I smiled at the young man and nodded forgivingly.

But then, as if my legs were a wild horse beyond my control, I ran after him. He took off like lightning, slipped, almost fell, then recovered. I pursued. We tore along the embankment. I ran like the wind and it was marvellous, a test for my legs. He was young, yet I closed in on him fairly easily, lifted the cudgel and with appalling violence swiped at his legs. Under my breath I murmured, what is your name, please forgive me! I struck at him again, muttering, take the coat, whoever you are, and the money, perhaps you need it! With all my strength I hit him a third time, saying, my behaviour is criminal and unforgivable! Then I let him go. I watched him limp up the long staircase to the street and disappear.

I went back remorsefully to my bench and decided that this time, whoever it was, I would let my coat be stolen. I spoke to my legs and right arm and reproached them with severity.

I walked along the bank and came to a place where steps led down to the water. I descended these steps and turned to look back. The bench was quite far away but the coat was still visible. I was lower now, smaller and less intimidating. Who would be the lucky one? I scanned the bank for signs of life. No one was in sight.

Then I must have slipped, because the next thing I knew I was in the water.

The water was cold and almost immediately I was out of my depth. I let go and went under. Gasping for breath I came up and began swimming. But I was caught up in a surprisingly powerful current. From the bank Old Father Tiber did not look dangerous at all. The water was muddy and looked sluggish. But this was deceptive.

I thought, what a silly way to die, after so much trouble. I would not have the chance to publish, to become a millionaire and be a philanthropist … But MM, of course, would soon tell the whole story. Lucy, who had shares in the company, would become rich. The water was really very cold and the current was pulling me under. Rome flashed past on both sides. I saw little Victor and his mother, tea in Kenwood and the picture of Andres. I held Lucy once more in my arms and her gentle voice sounded in my ears. I said goodbye.

And then my toe touched. There was solid ground beneath my feet. The water flung me against a wall. I inched around it, my feet entangled in weeds. Now the water was receding. I spat out mouthfuls of mud and fell, half unconscious, onto steps. When I came to I saw that I was on the island. The little island in the Tiber where there is a hospital and a monastery. I crept along for a while, then straightened up, and sighed; I was alive, though very cold. I shook myself like a dog and dried myself on an old newspaper.

I stumbled slowly across the bridge and back down to the bank. People saw me but paid no attention. It was quite a long way to the bench where my overcoat still lay, carefully folded. Nobody had taken it. Even the 300 euros were still in the pocket.

As best I could I made my way back to the hotel, my dripping clothes and shivering flesh concealed under the coat. Next day I had a sore throat, but no sign of pneumonia. I didn't mind too much – it was an adventure, after all.

18

I went straight back to Castir. It was easy to get there; a short plane journey from Rome, followed by an hour's ride on a local bus. Before long, with a sense of homecoming, I saw the Castir mountain looming on the horizon.

I enjoy taking public transport; it is a pleasure to sit incognito among ordinary people, while knowing that I am not ordinary at all.

But if I spend too long with my 'fellow humans' I begin to find them irritating; narrow-minded as they are, and obsessed with petty concerns.

They seem to me then like stuffed creatures: dolls in a dolls' house. I soon want to shut up the dolls' house and leave them to their own devices. Before doing telo I never thought of people in this way. The old Victor was quite the opposite. He entered all too willingly into the lives of others, sympathising with their emotions and desires. He was over-sensitive to other people, and, what's more, minded too much what they thought of him.

It was early afternoon. I walked up the path to the car park, where one other car was parked near the Cayman. This was rare, and it annoyed me; I wanted solitude.

But the joy of a camper van is that it can be moved.

A rough track leads from the car park to a higher level. Luckily the Cayman has big tyres and effective four-wheel drive. The engine started up immediately, although I had not driven it for some time. With some difficulty, for the Cayman is a large vehicle, I negotiated this rutted track; and at last reached a spot about one hundred metres above the car park. From here there is a spectacular drop to the river; it is vertical.

I parked near the edge, where a semi-circle of stones warns wanderers not to stray too close. The stones were loose and half broken; the local council would hardly bother to replace them, this far up the mountain. It was all but inaccessible. There was just room for the Cayman.

I switched off the engine and came out of the van. I sat beyond the stones, my feet dangling over the precipice. I felt no anxiety, no trace of vertigo. This I duly noted: old Victor was prone to vertigo, and avoided going close to steep drops.

Evening was approaching; already the sun was no more than a crescent above the horizon, and the sky was darkening fast. An ilex tree and a few thorn bushes ringed the spot, and these glowed with a violet haze, as if expelling the dying light. My nostrils filled with the odour of wild herbs, and I breathed in deeply. In a few minutes it would be night.

A sudden gust of wind blew across my face; I felt my cheeks tingle, and my hair ruffled. It was growing chilly, and I didn't want to catch a cold. I was human, after all.

So I went inside the van, lit the oil lamp and sat at my table. I would continue my work, the story of my life, the account of one man's victory over time.

And I started, on another page, to make notes for an article in the *Lancet*.

◆◆

But the wind grew stronger. The Cayman was buffeted by rough blasts, and I found I wasn't concentrating on my writing. What's more, I was hungry. So I swallowed a salami sausage I had brought back from Rome, and a packet of cream crackers. Then I put on my overcoat and a warm scarf, and went outside.

I love walking on the hillside in a storm. I looked up and hoped for lightning.

The chestnut trees were already in leaf, and their heavy branches swayed violently from side to side as I passed beneath them; it was almost dangerous. So, just in case, I kept to the path. I made my way down, past the car park and the river, and soon found myself crossing the amphitheatre behind the house. Lucy would be pleased, I thought. We'd both been away, and hadn't seen each other for some time.

As I opened the door, rain splashed onto my cheeks. Torrents of water began to fall from the sky, whipped by the wind into horizontal sheets.

Inside, although it was early, Lucy was upstairs in bed. I climbed to the bedroom and greeted her with a kiss. I told her I had been to Rome.

She nodded, and said, 'Would you like to hear about our concerts? We had a great success.'

'I'm sure you did,' I replied.

'Niko played marvellously. We had standing ovations.'

'And well deserved, I'm sure.'

I went to the window of the bedroom and looked out at the storm. I watched for quite a long time. Gradually the wind dropped, the rain eased and stars appeared.

'It's going to be a beautiful day tomorrow,' I said.

Lucy sighed. 'Poor Niko,' she said.

'Why poor?'

'He is lonely,' she went on. 'He never sleeps with anyone, he told me.'

'Perhaps he doesn't want to. He is a great musician. Don't women find that attractive?'

'He is too plump,' she said. 'Too soft. He has a big sagging belly. When I see him I can't help thinking of a piece by Eric Satie called "Music in the shape of a Pear".'

Personally I had always found Niko's playing very beautiful. When he drew his bow across the strings, he closed his eyes and his features were transformed. The sound he produced was unforgettable. To this day it resonates in my heart, from time to time. One completely forgot his unattractive physique.

Lucy herself had once said, 'It's as if an angel passes over his face.'

'Is he in love with you?' I asked.

'He might be,' she replied. 'If I responded. But I never could – even if I didn't have you, my darling.'

I tried hard to be jealous.

'You mind too much about appearance,' I told her. 'Youthful beauty, and all that.'

I undressed and went to bed. I curled up against Lucy, and almost fell asleep. But soon I felt her fingers probing my body. She still finds me irresistible, I thought. I kissed her, became partially aroused, and with some difficulty pushed myself inside her. But I kept popping out and had to start again. Rather like stuffing a last pair of socks into the washing machine, the thought occurred to me.

What's more, MM suddenly rushed into my mind, and I couldn't get rid of him. Publish, Victory, publish! he seemed to be saying, and I had a vision of his distrustful round eyes. I had the unpleasant feeling that those gelatine blobs would surface and pursue me whenever things were going well.

As I moved inside Lucy, I spoke silently to MM.

Dear old friend, I said, what a confused mishmash of ideas goes rolling about in your brain! I must say, in all honesty, that the successes we have had were to an extent due to you. I was, I have always been, full of admiration. I was sorry, of course, when you declined to come along with me on the telo adventure. I thought we would take off together, into the future. I thought the adventure would be very much to your taste.

After all it was you who first quoted to me Jim Watson's words: If we do not play God – who will?

Yet you had 'religious' scruples. Of course you have always been full of inconsistencies. You seemed half mad and yet, despite your youth, wise in a way not found in entirely sane people. You were not much interested in talking about scientific matters, but preferred discussing sex and recounting your experiences.

Animals, we once joked, would never need telo. Only humans, poor creatures with too big a brain, were conscious of their fate. They would die, and in the meantime they were small separate blobs desperate for re-connection.

But now, you see, all that is not quite relevant. For the past, with its dilemmas, its empathy, its mirror neurons, and the violent search for love – all this has lost its pull, though I remember it perfectly. My life is no longer a straight line stretching ever more feebly into the distance. It is, naturally, sometimes confusing. I look in the mirror and find myself hard to believe.

Is this me? Am I in control of this? It's as if I was being invented by someone else.

What sort of person would invent me? The answer is – everyone. Everyone would dream of being me. For everyone secretly wants to turn the world upside down, everyone is looking for a drastic solution, everyone knows in their heart that there is something wrong, no one can really accept resignation as the best possible answer.

Remember your great imaginative feats? You were Akira, a young woman with tresses of black hair reaching to your waist. A Mongol chieftain invaded your village, killed your parents and carried you off. For days you resisted him fiercely, and one night you stole his dagger and tried to kill him. But the chieftain slept with one eye open. He leapt up and a tremendous fight ensued, for you were strong as a man. I remember all the details (slightly different with each telling), my memory blossoms like a forest. At the last moment, when victory was within your grasp, you flung the dagger away. The chieftain ordered you to be bound hands and feet to his bed. You lay spread-eagled, preferring to die than to kill. The chieftain ordered his followers away. Blood dripping from his leg he knelt beside you. And then a remarkable change occurred. The bloodthirsty bandit became a man of infinite gentleness. With his rough hands he gradually set your body aflame. What began as a rape became a night of blissful passion.

As you told me this story your voice sank to a whisper and your eyes grew fixed. Oh what abandon! But now age has tamed you. Are you better off living domestically in a neat little house in Muswell Hill? Or better off stripped naked and tenderly robbed by a handsome vagabond in a Moscow park?

Shall I poison you? Concoct a subtle venom in the lab, perhaps using radioactive material. Or invite you to Castir and push you off the cliff? Or, better, have you sleep in the room beside the leaking stove pipe. But that would be foolish – don't you think? To risk ten years in prison – just as things are going well.

Simpler just to wait until you die.

This monologue lasted several minutes. With a last, forceful push I pretended to have an ebullient orgasm; and then Lucy and I lay exhausted, side by side.

Later I woke with a start and found myself beside my sleeping wife. First light was creeping through the window panes. My heart was beating fast. Lucy's thin bony body was radiating heat. The pillows swelled around her face, obstructing her breathing.

I counted her breaths, approximately five every ten seconds. That was 1,800 per hour, 43,200 per day. My mind was quick. 43,200 per day, 13,000,000 per year. In a lifetime perhaps one billion breaths. Not many, it seemed, for a lifetime. Only just a billionaire, in breaths. Every hour that passed L. was nearer death by 1,800.

I had a moment of panic, the old fear of time the murderer. I lay still, trying to quieten my heart. How many heartbeats in a lifetime? Lucy's face was squashed by the pillow, straining for breath. I touched her cheek.

CHRISTOPHER OSBORN

I had not told her about telomerase, or the treatment. She knew nothing of what I was doing. I raised myself above her and breathed on her face. She turned away. My arms felt strong and light. Suddenly my body roared with unusual vigour, vitality coursed through me like a charge. And it seemed to me that this charge would burn to a cinder the little body beneath me. But Lucy slept on fearless, her breath now quiet and deep.

I pulled down the duvet a little and carefully extracted her hand. L's hands are broad, large for her size, the fingers rather short. Victor affectionately called them workman's hands. Now I held the hand. Even in the dim light it showed signs of age. The fingertips looked flatter and softer, the skin around the knuckles bunched, the veins and tendons clearly visible. What a piece of work is a hand! Motionless now, in an instant these fingers could fly over the piano keys, effortlessly controlling the mechanism. I wondered if age was gradually reducing that magical ability.

I kissed the hand; then, as if rising from the grave, slipped quietly and rapidly out of bed. I left a note, and went out into the dawn landscape, Castir.

♦♦

I took the path that leads behind the amphitheatre and bounded up the hillside. Dear old Victor loved this path, sometimes imagining that it was known only to him and the red deer. The path was steep and stony and Victor used to take his time, examining animal tracks and taking samples of plants he did not recognise.

But now I was propelled in an instant up the mountain, not at all out of breath. From rock to rock I leapt and soon the village and the olive groves were far below. I stood poised on a patch of stiff grass as if to take off into the valley. Upsurges of warm air swept over my chest and outstretched arms. Light as the air itself I stood, yet strong, massive, my feet planted like trees in the earth. I took off my shirt and tied it round my waist. I would roam half naked, away from the paths, wild as an animal, untamed. The sun was rising into a sky of palest blue, and I was alone. I wanted to cry out; my face cracked open into a smile so wide that my cheeks ached.

I don't think old Victor ever experienced anything like this. For he was afraid of solitude, you see. All his life he craved company, continually, desperately trying to please others, to be loved. He never faced the fundamental quality, the baseline of existence. Now I stood on the hillside and watched the sun rise and the mist disperse, the shadows in the hollows, the distant olive plantations and the toy houses huddling in the valley which was still dark. Around me animals were waking and below my feet insects and countless microbes were endlessly at work. How beautiful, how impersonal it was! Old Victor never faced this: aloneness. He needed balm, consolation, warmth. But now I stood exhilarated, eyes wide. My feet sank like roots to the deep core of the earth.

And what is gone, have I lost anything? One thing perhaps: the old craving – but for what? – the vague sense of dissatisfaction that persisted, some melancholy dissatisfaction, no matter how happy, how successful I was, the sense that something – but what? – was somewhere lacking, in life itself … Well, this old craving is no more.

I laugh out loud. I am content with myself. I remember everything about the past, the words, the facts – though not the feeling itself; yes, not the feeling – does it matter? I mean, I write the words, they are the correct words, but I can't really put myself back into the shoes of Victor so long ago – that fear, fragility, fog and hope. But would I want to?

And music – how does that fit in?

I haven't told Lucy, but music, at present, no longer has quite the same effect on me. When I hear L. practising the piano, repeating the same passages, I sometimes refer to it (privately) as 'noise'. Whereas before, I was thrilled, almost overawed, to have a real pianist working in the house. I would listen outside the door to the way she dissected the music, trying out phrases at different speeds and dynamics, and then bringing the whole piece together again. And my delight increased, at first, after starting telo.

But gradually I have become more engrossed by the experiment itself, by myself and my own body. At night I dream of the reconstruction taking place inside me – I dream of ruins, of walking among decrepit buildings, and timbers and stone slabs fall around me, with a roar sometimes so loud it wakes me up. Or I am walking in a neon city; its streets are the glowing arms of the double helix. Shielding my eyes I am dazzled by an army of coloured lights.

I went back to the Cayman where it sat, unblemished, in its new location. It bore no sign of the winds that had rocked it the night before. Twigs and branches, brought down by the storm, lay across the ground.

I entered the Cayman, and it welcomed me. I was happy in the van; I worked better here and slept better. The bed was narrow and quite hard; but who needs luxury?

19

My pen has run out. Just now, as I wrote the last words. I touch the drawer beneath the table top and it springs open. In the Cayman everything functions well. Not only the vehicle itself but everything in it glides on wheels. Of course I have a computer here (two actually) but I like writing by hand. My pen has run out, so I feel among the objects in the drawer. My sense of touch is sharp. I find a pencil and rub the shiny green paint between thumb and forefinger, the ridged hexagonal cylinder.

I hold the pencil aloft and pause. I wonder where to go, what to say. I could lie down and rest; after all I didn't sleep much last night. But I am not tired.

The pencil itself gives me an idea.

Sometimes I like to remember the distant past, and my memory never fails me.

I bring the pencil down onto a new white sheet of paper, and write, in my all but illegible handwriting: On the Merits of Dying.

I smiled to myself; there was a pleasant irony in the words.

Then I continued, a few lines below:

As a boy at school we had a new chemistry teacher.

He was a funny little man with wisps of white hair which stuck up all over his head like whipped cream. He was called Trevor Fish, which caused us children a good deal of amusement. He was universally known as Chips.

One day Chips gave us a rather good lesson. He stood in

front of the class and said, in his squeaky, slightly pompous voice: 'Has anybody got a pencil?'

A ripple of barely suppressed giggles passed from desk to desk. We all pretended to look, urgently, in our pockets, under our desks, all over the floor, in the rubbish bin, and on the shelves, for a pencil. But nobody found one.

When the commotion died down Chips said, 'This does not surprise me. Most of us have pens of course. Biros, felt tips. Pens which leak, covering us with ink, and run out. We daub our exercise books with ink, and cross out our mistakes, and our work becomes illegible. With a pencil, all you need is a rubber. What is a rubber, by the way? What is *rubber?* Yes, some of you know, I expect, rubber comes from trees. That is an interesting story, the story of the rubber tree, the Amazon jungle and the perfidy of an Englishman. But what *is* rubber? I mean – what is the chemical composition of rubber? Well, we'll do that another day. Today is the day of the pencil.'

From the pocket of his tweed jacket, which was lopsided and shapeless and resembled a crumpled blanket, Chips took a bright yellow pencil. He had a habit of producing unexpected objects, like a magician, from his pockets. Now he held up the pencil between thumb and forefinger as if he had performed a trick, and we laughed.

Ships, said Chips, bring materials from all over the world to be eventually assembled into the little writing stick that we never bother to think about at all. The best pencils, Chips told us, are made from the wood of the Incense Cedar tree. This tree is evergreen, and grows in temperate habitats. In the wild it can live for a thousand years. Ever heard of it? No? Well, it makes the best pencils. [Laughter.] And the lead of the pencil? It is not lead but graphite, and comes mostly from China. Graphite is pure carbon, and so is a diamond. But diamond is the hardest substance known, and graphite is one of the softest. What makes the difference? The way the atoms are arranged. Same atoms, different arrangement. That's all. Chemistry. The pencil is machined into a hexagonal, and then painted. What is paint? Chemically rather complex, said Chips. A balance of different molecules. Et cetera. Chemistry. There is nothing else.

Little Victor was spellbound.

And you and I have been similarly assembled from common elements in the air and the earth and, according to proportion and subtle arrangement, turned into considerably differing individuals. Nature is impersonal. Swallow an antibiotic – a poison made by a bacterium – and your pneumonia, caused by a different bacterium, is cured. Two atoms of oxygen and one of carbon make carbon dioxide, the basis of all life on the planet; but one of oxygen and one of carbon make carbon monoxide, which will kill you.

The study of the colossal squid, of Pauline's illness, and even the miraculous way she began to recover – this too fell within the domain of chemistry. And I myself, I began to understand, was a machine of vast complexity, yet made of simple elements, related in direct and undreamt-of ways to every other living organism on the planet.

Little Victor made a solemn pledge: to dedicate himself, when he grew up, to the curing of illness, the relief of poverty and misery, and the general betterment of mankind – through science.

Meanwhile, as Chips was delivering his magnificent lesson, he had a flashback. There he was, a child having tea with his mother on Hampstead Heath. He was in a bad mood – she wouldn't let him have another cake; I can see precisely the little chocolate and walnut cakes he loved. He was grumpy and scowling but his mother took no notice. She was smiling at him, in her usual dreamy way. Then she murmured, as if speaking to herself: 'Do you remember Andres?'

I was only thinking of the cake I wanted. But still, the name Andres struck me, and seemed a lovely, intriguing name. Was that the first time I had heard it? Perhaps. The name Andres blended in my mind with the little chocolate and walnut cake, sweet and crisp. Soon afterwards I discovered in our attic the biology textbook in a strange language, and then the photograph of a young man with a pale angular face. But I continued to picture him, at the same time, as small, brown and crisp, like the walnut cake.

20

I could spend all my time in the Cayman, on the Castir hillside. It's where I feel most at home.

But I still have my flat in London. And I have to put in an occasional appearance at the lab. I don't stay there very long. I check up on the work my researchers are doing, and sometimes put in a few remarks. Then I leave them to get on with it. I like to wander the streets of the overpopulated city, and watch all the haggard souls rushing about their business.

One day, in my roaming, I found myself at the place on Camden Road, where little Victor had once played with Vivian, his hero, the black boy who was such a master roller-skater.

It was early summer, and beautiful weather.

But there was no sign of the playground, or the raised ramps where I learnt how to skate. Instead there were three tall council blocks and a patch of grass. I raised my eyebrows in mock surprise. I walked around for a bit, smiling at the names on the blocks: Babylon, Bethlehem, Nazareth. On an impulse I went into Babylon and climbed to the seventh floor. I didn't take the lift; the stairs would be good exercise, I thought.

Up on the seventh floor I surveyed the gloomy array of doors. Why the seventh? No particular reason. Being a little out of breath I sat down on the concrete walkway. There was nobody else there. Vaguely I watched, through the railing, children playing on the grass below. I sank into a reverie and remembered the hours I had spent as a boy in the same place, before the council block was built, with my roller skates. Perhaps it was the happiest time of my life, I thought. But it was also a time of suffering, for there I had lost Vivian. One day he wasn't there and never came back.

I must have dropped off, for suddenly somebody was standing in front of me and trying to open the door I was leaning against. I got to my feet and said stupidly: 'I'm sorry – I was looking for Vivian.'

A young black woman smiled at me. She was large; not tall or fat, but dense. She was wearing a rather short skirt, with no socks or tights, and red shoes.

She said, with a slight foreign accent: 'Who is it you're looking for?'

'Vivian.'

'You're on the wrong floor. There's no Vivian on this floor.' Then her face brightened. 'I'll be Vivian. Is that what you'd like? I'll be your Vivian for you.'

I felt dizzy and stepped back against the railing.

The memory of my childhood days, and of the boy Vivian twisting and leaping like an elf; and the time when he fell and lay on the bench with his head in my lap (an invention, I think) – the memory of all this was suddenly very sharp. I turned away and held the railing. Immediately the woman was at my side and her arm was around me.

'You're not well,' she murmured in the gentlest voice. 'Come inside and I'll give you a cup of tea.'

She opened the door of her flat and we went in.

It was a cramped, crowded sort of place. Her sitting room was full of all kinds of odd objects. They were hard to make out at first, because the curtains were drawn. But then I began to see them clearly; they were puppets. Miniature women in black skirts and braids, like Mexicans, stared out from shelves, china figures of shepherds and milkmaids, stocky plaster peasants in heavy clogs, and many others. They seemed carefully arranged, some turned towards each other as if in conversation.

'Where on earth did you get all this?' I asked.

'Oh, I picked them up,' she said, 'here and there.'

Leaning against one wall I saw a strange object, like a primitive musical instrument. It was a simple wooden box, with three metal strings spanning the wood, loosely attached at each end.

'What is that?' I asked, pointing at it.

'That's a wind harp,' she answered immediately. 'You hang it up in the wind and it plays itself. Never seen one before?'

I made my way through the densely scattered objects and picked up the wind harp. It was surprisingly heavy; the wooden boards were thick and crudely stuck together. I could feel bubbles of dried glue sticking out along the sides. I tried twanging the strings, but the sound was dull and without resonance.

'There's no room for it here,' she said. 'You're a musician. Would you like it?'

'But I'm not a musician.'

'I thought of putting it up outside the flat,' she went on. 'But if the wind blew it would scare the neighbours! So it's just sitting in here. You can take it with you. It's got another name, a lion harp, or Ealing harp, something like that.'

An Ealing harp? Something stirred in my memory.

'Do you mean an Aeolian harp?'

Was that not also the name of a piece by Chopin?

'I'll leave it here,' I said, putting the harp back down against the wall.

Beside it, in the corner, lay the skull of a deer-like creature, with grinning teeth intact; next to it an antler, half covered in dark peeling skin. These came, she said, from the Amazon, Brazil. The way she said Brazil hit me; there was a softness, a lilt in her pronunciation. Was she too from Brazil?

Oh yes, she said, how did you guess?

Immediately I began to tell her about Andres. Looking at me with the eyes of a clairvoyant she nodded repeatedly and said, 'I'm sure of it, darling. It was Andres – your daddy. You see, you're Brazilian like me.'

I began to tell her everything; my life poured out. From the very first I felt completely at ease and talked to her as if talking to myself. I told her about telo – in a way I had not yet done with Lucy. I told Vivian about it without difficulty, for nothing surprised her. I told her of our amazing discovery, the formula that enabled us to control the production of telomerase. I told her that this discovery would change the future of mankind. I told her about Castir, the mountain and the nature reserve. I told her that I was a happy man, a lucky man, and that I was an addict.

'Oh, we're all addicts,' she said. 'What's yours?'

'Nothing really,' I replied. 'Just telo.'

Laughing I said that some people would call me a drug addict, in the power of those little plastic bottles I kept in the fridge in my study.

She took me in her arms and kissed my head. An extraordinary warmth came from her body, like electricity, passing through her clothes. Then she let go and said, 'What a great story. You're so lucky to be doing something important. What you're doing is important for everybody. It's a world adventure!' She added, 'So let's celebrate. I'll make cocktails.'

From behind the deer skull on the floor she took a bottle of rum. She fetched lime and sugar and ice, and made caipirinhas. It's my favourite, she confided. I sat close to her, basking in her warmth.

For a long time we said nothing. Then I felt the glass slipping from my hand and my eyes closing.

Vivian had a great capacity for silence. There was a kind of animal intimacy between us, and words seemed an interruption. After a while, however, I sat up and asked her what she did.

She answered, 'I am a physiotherapist.'

I regretted asking this, it was a kind of reflex politeness. For now she was rousing herself from that animal torpor, which was so agreeable. She cleared her throat and began mumbling indistinctly: '… not today, but that is what I do sometimes, physiotherapy, but today is Thursday and I always do something else on Thursday afternoon. I go to the school and pick up my son. You see, I have a son, Jacob, and there was nothing wrong with him today, he was happy to see me as he always is, and he is growing up now, twelve years old, he is nearly a teenager and the years have passed so fast, and I have not been a proper mother ...'

'Why?' I asked, and again regretted it; for the fact was, I wanted to know as little as possible about Vivian, so that she could be completely a creature of my imagination, like her living room, like the puppets. More than ever this was what I wanted, I realised – to shape people, to create them.

But I persisted, 'Why have you not been a proper mother?'

And at that moment I, who had no children, felt for a second the old desire once again, which long ago had passed, the desire to be a father.

'Because I am not, I am not stable,' she said. 'If that is the right word. They say I am not – reliable.'

I was almost pleased to hear this; I did not want her to be stable. I wanted her, as far as possible, to remain vague, formless, hardly a person at all.

She continued, '... and I was accused of so many unfair things, even of being a prostitute, but I have never taken money, believe me –'

'But even if you had,' I put in, 'what business is it of anybody else?'

'And my mother took Jacob, with that bitch of a husband, and I am not allowed to see him, not much ...' Tears poured from her eyes, and I too felt something happening; my heart cracked open a little, even though I didn't want all these revelations. Suddenly I thought of Lucy. For a moment I longed for Lucy; I saw her eyes, heard her voice.

Vivian got up quickly. 'I have to take my medication,' she said in a subdued voice, and left the room. Later, in the bathroom, I looked at her pills; she was an epileptic. On the little bottle from the pharmacy, the date and a name were printed: Miss B. Murray. But I didn't care what the B stood for. For me she was Vivian.

When she came back her mood had changed. She was cheerful and said she would cook us something nice, her mother had taught her to cook well. I asked how often she saw her son, but she shook her head and placed her fingers on my lips. After dinner and a bottle of wine we watched a good movie, *Exterminating Angel*, an old favourite of mine.

◆◆

'I must go,' I said.

'Oh no,' she replied. 'You're far too drunk.'

'I'm sorry. I've stayed too long.'

'No, you haven't. The fact is,' she continued, with a kind of natural directness, 'the fact is, you're my type. I like older men.'

I didn't take this as a compliment; after all, I was trying not to be an older man. I had told her about the experiment, but perhaps she hadn't been listening. Never mind, I thought. If she prefers me as a decomposing seventy-year-old, so be it.

'You're droll,' she said.

'Droll?'

'Yes, you've got a funny face.'

Slowly she began to undress me, loosening my shirt and my trouser belt; and I put up no resistance. She took off her own blouse, and lay beside me. There was a blanket on one arm of the sofa, and this she pulled over us. I can see the blanket clearly in my mind's eye; it was thick, a little rough, and embroidered with llamas from South America.

She hugged me, and I lay like a child, warmed and protected. We lay like this without moving, for perhaps half an hour, and then Vivian began to press against me. She took my hand and put it on her breast. Her breath quickened, she began to gasp, and writhed against me in a kind of frenzy. I think she had an orgasm straightaway. Then she lifted her skirt and without pausing took my penis and put it inside her. She was wearing no underwear.

I was fully aroused; there was no trace of the impotency I had been suffering with Lucy. And so we made love, she cried out, and quickly it was over.

A few moments later I could tell from her breathing that she was asleep. I lay still, in a state of repose. A smile stretched across my face from cheek to cheek. There is nothing more depressing for a man than to feel that his sexual ability is failing; now, with Vivian, I seemed to have recovered this ability. Would it last? As I lay in the darkness I touched my genitals. My penis was soft now, childlike, but might it rouse itself again?

My eyes were open but a haze seemed to cover my vision at first. Then the haze evaporated, and I saw where I was very clearly: the stuffy little room, overlaid with objects of all kinds. And above me, pulled up to my chin, was a colourful blanket.

But now I could hardly believe what was happening.

In the depths of the night the miniature figures on shelves and tables began to come to life. They were taking over. Vivian's sleeping breath seemed to pass into them, their clothes began to rustle and with tiny clicks and creaks they stirred arms and legs. And gradually, the silence grew full of underground whispers. I looked over to where the Aeolian harp lay, the wind harp, a darker shape against the wall. Would it too come to life and begin to whine softly?

I remember the first time little Victor put a drop of muddy water on a slide and looked at it through a microscope, and saw all the squirming creatures, as real as anything in the visible world. Just like that, just as the drop of pond water was filled with life under the microscope, I now watched the miniature figures move and rustle while Vivian slept. The secret life, I thought; the life of the body. For I could almost feel the rustling inside me of that unreachable part of myself, the DNA within my cells, the hidden factory, and I thought with sudden fear, what am I doing, what will happen to me? What am I, what have I done?

Immediately, as if to console me, it seemed that my mother

was sitting beside me; my mother of the last years, when she lost the use of words and her laughter and vitality were gone, her expression fearful or blank; that time of anguish when she could no longer tell me about Andres, or anything in the world. Yet now she was saying: I am with you in your adventure, you will come through, never forget, I am with you, you will succeed. You are a scientist. An innovator. I trust you.

Together, my mother beside me, we watched and listened; then I must have fallen asleep.

When I awoke, it was another day. The curtains were glowing, my mother was gone, and the puppets were lifeless.

I was on the edge of the sofa, and restless. I began to get hot, and stood up. Vivian was lying on her back, her breath now very quiet. I looked carefully at her. Even in her sleep she radiated kindness.

She was not as young as I thought. Her face was broad and fleshy and her eyebrows, which were quite thick, sloped downwards. She seemed to be smiling, as if she could see me through her eyelids. I pulled a face to check, but she didn't stir.

I went to the bathroom, and couldn't help looking at my body. The return of potency was not, it appeared, the only change. Both knees now looked smooth! But my hands were still uneven: one old and spotted and the other fresh. My neck was slack. On my right foot, but not on the left, the toenails were yellow and a prey to fungus infection.

As I write now, my neck is still a little loose but I am optimistic. The central fold is gradually re-absorbing. And my toenails are clear.

But back then, in Vivian's bathroom, I had a second's shudder. I was piecemeal. I was patchwork.

I spoke consolingly to myself: My dear Victor – what do you expect? No great advance has been made by humanity without trouble. You're the prototype. Prototypes tend to be a little ropey. Relax. Wouldn't it be worse if you were old all over?

I went back into the sitting room, where Vivian was still

asleep. I made my way carefully through the objects on the floor to the Aeolian harp. In the dark I felt it all over with my fingers and palms. I rubbed the ridges of glue and pressed down the strings to make sure they wouldn't sound. Then I lifted the harp and held it against my chest. The wood was warm, almost as warm as Vivian herself. Hadn't she said she wanted to give it to me?

I felt grateful to Vivian. From her I hid nothing, needed to hide nothing; I was an open book.

Holding the harp under one arm, I kissed her on the forehead and slipped away. I think I almost loved her. Though I have never been back to see her. But I think she expected this and did not mind.

21

Invigorated by my night with Vivian, I decided to put my new-found virility to the test.

I could hardly be unaware of the lovely female forms that seemed to pop up everywhere, like fields of wild flowers.

I didn't want a 'love affair'. I couldn't imagine having to go through all the preliminaries (and after-liminaries), the small talk, the seduction, etc. What's more, I didn't want to have to explain my special situation. Nor did I want to have to lie about my age – what is it, anyway? I am not interested in lies and excuses. I almost envied gay men for whom it is easy to find sex in certain places, where strangers can devour each other in purest love, in whispers, without introduction. Experience rare for heteros. (Would we want it, would I want it?)

I am not interested in pretence. You see, I have become fearless. Sometimes, when talking to someone, I realise that my gaze is unflinching, and then I lower my eyes, for that is what people are used to. I do not want to shock them.

I went back to a house I had once known in a city in the South of France.

This is the oldest house in an old street. Crooked and leaning outwards it looks about to collapse, but has withstood six centuries or more. On the wall is a blue plaque which reads (I translate): The only surviving edifice of the ancient Rue des Mercières, which marked the former boundary between the Quartier des Mercières and the Quartier des Cordonniers. In plain English: the quarter of haberdashers and the quarter of shoemakers. This house was built in 1413 by François d'Yeu, and was used a storehouse for the confection of prunes and the distillation of liqueur.

In French the name of the builder, François d'Yeu, is suggestive; it sounds the same as François Dieu (François God). And it is also the name of a luminous windswept island, Ile d'Yeu.

In addition, there is an interesting phrase on the blue plaque. The words 'former boundary' are, in French: *La frontière d'antan*. I had to look up 'd'antan': my dictionary gives 'of yesteryear'. I felt I should take it as my own, my nom de plume, or nom de guerre – *Victor d'Antan*. It was like d'Artagnan, or Danton, the noble revolutionary, beheaded in his turn.

But Victor d'Antan stood in its own right: Victor of Yesteryear! You can see why I liked it. As for the haberdashers and cobblers, I'm not sure what their significance was. But that the house had once been used for the distillation of liqueur and the confection of prunes, was oddly appropriate.

One of the gifts of telo is that I seem able to lay claim not only to the future, but also the past. Before, if someone mentioned a date far ahead, I would think: well, anyway I won't be around then. But now I start to imagine vividly what the world might be like at that far-off time. And the same is true of the past. When I read that François d'Yeu built this house in 1413, the intervening years took off and exploded like a balloon. With no difficulty I could picture myself having a conversation with F. d'Yeu, a bewigged middle-aged gentleman in doublet and hose and buckled shoes. And with a blink, his tumble-down storehouse was restored to its pristine state.

Long ago Victor had found himself at the door of the Maison d'Yeu. He entered like a savage, behaved like a savage – not because Lucy had disappointed him, on the contrary; an old primitive urge occasionally drove him there, which had nothing to do with her. It was life itself that could not be neatly tied into a bundle.

In those days Victor might have found it quite easy to become addicted to the Maison d'Yeu; but he was far too busy. Also, I must say, I do not have an addictive nature. My present attraction to the drug telo is not an addiction; I could certainly give it up, if I chose. For I have always known that happiness depends on a judicious blending of different elements – love, work and play, as Freud said.

Sometimes, in his youth, Victor came to the Maison as if to meet friends and acquaintances – for the guests often reminded him of people he knew, and he named them accordingly. Mind you, he never spoke to them.

It was to this place that I now made my way.

A small white card was stuck to the door, with the words: Private Club.

I pressed the buzzer, was scrutinised through a square of one-way glass, and allowed in. There is a small entrance hall and vestiaire; beyond, a long zinc bar and round tables with velvet banquettes. It was just the same as before.

Monsieur and Madame were still behind the bar, withered, diminished, both with heavily dyed hair, scurrying to and fro, smoking themselves to perdition and serving delicious cocktails. Madame reminded me of those indestructible old ladies you see in French towns, wearing short dresses, taking moth-eaten little dogs for a walk. Privately I called her 'the poodle'. The old couple seemed to recognise me as I bobbed in and slipped onto one of the high stools.

'*Mais vous n'avez pas changé, Monsieur!*'

There is a preponderance of men, who sit quietly and keep their eyes on the door. When a woman enters, usually accompanied by a man, but occasionally – and thrillingly – alone, the men shift in their seats, greetings are exchanged and conversation begins to hum.

Steps lead down to the lower floors.

In the basement, three levels down, is the dance area. This

room is mirrored all round, except for a darkened area to one side with a large couch running from wall to wall.

The upper levels are furnished with sofas in alcoves and raised surfaces of different sizes. These surfaces are soft and well-upholstered, usually in velvet, apart from one large rectangular area which is covered in buttoned black leather. The leather squeaks slightly with the shifting of weight, and the buttons leave little red imprints, especially on pale skin. There is a kind of metal grille dividing this leather section in two, which reminds one of a fake dungeon. There are niches for clothes and working showers on each floor.

Some of the women who come here want as many men as they can get, without pausing from one to the next; and for this soft little benches by the wall serve as a kind of waiting area.

One of those who intrigued me was not young, by any means. She was rather tall, respectably dressed, with small rimless glasses. I saw her first on the dance floor, with a fat little man in a business suit. They danced decorously for quite a long time and then he began slipping his hand up her skirt.

Once again, as in the old days, many of these people whom I had never seen before looked very much like people I already knew. The couple on the dance floor, the little fat man and the older woman, reminded me immediately of Celestina and Arturo, two acquaintances in Castir.

Arturo ran the post office, but his great interest was hunting. In the shooting season he spent many hours tracking birds on the mountainside with his dog, a cocker spaniel named Pluto. Sometimes for days on end the post office remained, most annoyingly, closed.

Celestina, on the other hand, was the intellectual of the village. She was a founder member of our concert society, and had a romantic attachment to the Park. Unmarried and childless she was the local historian of the area, and her photographs and drawings adorned the pages of our guide books. She liked nothing better than to sleep on the mountainside in a tent and take pictures at dawn. Her knowledge of the mountain was unrivalled. She was a conservationist, and heartily disliked Arturo, especially for his hunting and shooting. If she needed the post office she preferred to avoid him and go to the next village.

Yet here were their doubles on the dance floor, he with his hand up her skirt, she lavishing saliva on his pasty cheeks.

Once the dancing was over, Celestina led Arturo by the hand to a higher level. She took up a prostrate position on a couch and carefully removed her spectacles. She became insatiable, and fat little Arturo was soon dealt with. He lay quietly to one side, his hairy belly spilling over the velvet.

Celestina was a tigress; she liked variety and was impatient with long stayers. '*Ne sois pas egoiste,*' I heard her murmur to one, who was having trouble reaching orgasm. She lay with her mouth ajar, and her movements were small but suggestive, a slight rotation of the hips, slow opening and closing of her thighs; and once, having despatched a young pink gorilla I named Orlando (after a new researcher at our lab), raised herself languidly onto elbows and knees and lifted high her long posterior. Dropping her head into the padded surface she let out a series of high staccato yelps.

Celestina was fussy about the spots she chose. She only liked two of the alcoves (both with purple lighting), and if one of these was not available she would return to the dance floor. She never went onto the leather surface. I think she disliked the squeaks and did not want the imprint of the buttons on her skin.

At precisely nine fifteen a bell rings from upstairs. This is an old-fashioned brass bell which Madame shakes at the top of the steps. It is sometimes the subject of discussion. Madame finds the bell heavy nowadays (she suffers from arthritis) and wonders if it can be heard clearly enough on the lower levels.

The clanging brass indicates that dinner is ready – and very good it is. A rectangular wooden table fills the room and the food is laid out in sumptuous style. The guests come quickly upstairs, after dressing. The wine is excellent and unlimited. At weekends there are candles on little green saucers.

In the background, never too loud, there is music. Usually popular French songs from the old days, classics in their way; but once it was the piece by Chopin called the 'Aeolian Harp'. I have heard you play it, Lucy. The music blew across the dining table like wind singing in the trees.

And, as I ate, I remembered: I had an Aeolian harp of my own, a present from Vivian. A wind harp. While the other diners made conversation, I began to work out a location for its strange music.

This banquet reminds me of the lunches we used to have in Castir, to discuss our music festival. We would set up a long trestle table in our garden under the walnut trees. The mayor came, with his secretary, any musicians or artists we could find, shopkeepers, park wardens; and the real Celestina and Arturo, who always sat as far away as possible from each other.

Here in the Maison d'Yeu the dinners are much shorter, of course, they are an interlude. But there is a similar spirit of conviviality. Everything tastes better than usual, and there is plenty of high-spirited talk. Some people are surprisingly unchanged by the addition of clothes; others utterly.

Celestina and Arturo sit together and eat like wolves, though politely. Arturo has small pointed teeth, hers are long and uneven. I imagine them discussing the wildlife in Castir.

After coffee most people return downstairs.

◆◆

Celestina gave Arturo a loud kiss on the lips, and made her way to the lower levels. Arturo remained at the bar, chatting to Monsieur and Madame. I followed Celestina.

She took off her clothes, and lay down in one of her favourite spots.

It seemed to me that the décor on these lower levels had been updated. The lighting, I thought, was more subtle, with small spots sunk in the ceiling and walls. And there were more mirrors.

At least, that was my impression. In the old days I had not been much interested in mirrors. But now, as I watched Celestina and her playmates in the purple alcove, there were mirrors all round.

Before dinner I had hardly noticed this. But now, with my senses pleasantly blurred, I relaxed and examined my surroundings more closely.

I undressed and left my clothes in one of the niches provided. And then I couldn't help catching my reflection in the mirror walls.

It was an opportunity to check up on myself. On the right of my head, I saw that there were still patches of white in my hair, not around the ears, but higher, towards the crown. However on the left side, there was no white to be seen.

Lowering my gaze over the rest of my body I rather screwed up my eyes at first. But then I saw that my general outline was not bad at all. Bending forward, my stomach did not suddenly pop out like a jelly – but my breasts, especially the one on the right, were still a little pendulous. Turning my back to the mirror I tensed my buttocks and checked the creases. A fuzz of hair was creeping up from the thigh over the left globe, but not on the right. I couldn't remember if this had been the case when young.

But there were small tufts of hair, left and right, on my shoulder blades. I didn't like this and it was definitely new; I had always had a smooth back. Thinking there might be some discolouration on the glass I rubbed it with my moistened finger, but then I saw the hair clearer than ever, though less black than the hair on my head; and now, as I write, there is also a covering on the back of my hand and the finger joints, not coarse like an ape, but quite fine, though thickish.

Just as I was trying to come to terms with this – the first tufts of hair on my back – there was a commotion behind me and pink Orlando pushed past. At the same time Celestina, groaning in the alcove, suddenly gave a big smile and beckoned to me. Perhaps, I thought crazily, she has recognised me. Perhaps she really was the Celestina I knew in Castir? Her smile was surprisingly charming. I had a clear view of her long worn-away teeth. I remembered that, whatever else, telo could not repair teeth – mine would soon be like hers. I saw Celestina's hands – they were old; strong, masculine hands, veined and covered in brown spots.

This reassured me; it was definitely not the Castir Celestina, who was younger and whose hands were unspotted.

I advanced slowly towards this elderly lady who lay so naked in the alcove. I could feel the beauty of my invigorated figure; and I took a few steps towards her, aware that the rubbery folds in my neck had all but disappeared. I carefully patted my hair into place, pleased at its thickness. As I approached, my penis began to ready itself. Oh, the joy, to feel again the blood in my loins! No doubt about it. And with Celestina, of all people. I touched her thigh, which was encouragingly warm, and waited for her to seize hold of my manhood.

But instead she removed my fingers and retreated to the back of the alcove. Young Orlando pushed in front of me, somewhat roughly, and I felt the unpleasant sensation of his hairy legs rubbing past mine. Now I saw that Celestina's smile was directed not at me but at this pink gorilla. Orlando was quick to take up the invitation; and I stepped back.

Now it seemed that I stood alone in a pool of my own; all the others, men and women, seemed to recoil and give me a wide berth. Yet I stood straight and tall, unaware, when I glanced at myself, of any flaw in my appearance.

Fools, I said to myself.

The thought of Lucy flooded through me. I stood rooted between the mirrors and Lucy returned to me in her tenderness and beauty.

Was that why I returned to the Maison d'Yeu – to find L.? I did not think so, at the time. Yet the more I observed my fellow bipeds the more I thought longingly of Lucy. I came back again, several times in the following weeks. It was not hard to get there from Castir.

And still no one looked at me with eyes of desire. Even in this cramped dungeon, this lust-den, I was avoided and shunned. Why? It was inexplicable.

Oblivious to the behaviour of the others I concentrated on my physique, and examined myself in the multiple mirrors. And I was pleased by what I saw. Things were changing fast. It had taken time for telo to get going, but now the momentum was unstoppable.

The tufts on my back soon seemed more evenly spread, my breasts no longer hung forward, my buttocks filled out; and I could no longer make out any white hair on my head.

Unable to conceal a smile I watched the antics of the others. They were so predictable it was as if I was directing them myself. I fitted them with magnets and they lost control of themselves. They were sticky, incomplete, desperate – creatures in need. If there was nothing else, they would fling themselves against walls, doors, sofas, floors. Such was their need. Yet perhaps without need there is no 'love'?

Then I stopped going to the Maison d'Yeu. I said goodbye to Monsieur and Madame and they replied, as usual: '*A bientôt, cher Monsieur!*'

I was touched by their dedication, the warm welcome they gave to their guests, the excellent food they served.

I stepped into the street, a free man. It was raining. By the light of the street lamps I read the words on the blue plaque. My eyesight was excellent; I no longer had to peer close. I read again about François d'Yeu, who built the house in 1413, the distillation of liqueur, the confection of prunes. I was oddly exhilarated. My heart was thumping so hard it began to be painful. But why? It's because, I told myself, you are striking a new path, no one has been here before. But I was trembling. I thought: yes, telo. But what is it doing to you?

Why do the revellers here avoid you? Why do they not see you as you really are?

I shrugged; after all, it was their problem.

The door opened and out came Celestina and Arturo. I smiled; they were clearly regulars. I greeted them and they nodded politely. They walked off arm in arm under a large umbrella. They were old and almost bent double. Do they love each other? I wondered.

But what is telo doing to *you?* I'm really not sure. I could stop telo; and be like everyone else, sticky and hopeful.

It was two o'clock in the morning; despite the rain I was not cold, and my muscles were working perfectly. It's that time of the night, I thought – courage! The street was empty, C. and A. had disappeared, there were no others left.

I made my way back to my hotel with an easy step, humming an old tune from the past – an air from *Don Giovanni*, I think.

22

Lucy, all this is difficult to explain, please don't think of it as some kind of banal deception. If you knew what was happening to me, how troubled I had been by my loss of virility, I think you would not blame me for going to the Maison d'Yeu.

Also, I hadn't told you about what I was doing, about telo, because I was afraid you wouldn't accept it, and just said I was testing some new detox drug. But this avoidance grew every day like a snowball, divided us as we had never been divided, caused me to spend more and more time away from you, made me fear our reunions ...

And so I told you.

'I know,' you said.

Only one other person could have told you: MM.

'And I know it's dangerous,' you said.

To begin with, there was me and Lavinia. We always knew that our project incurred the risk of cancer. We hoped we had found a way of activating the telomerase gene that would not be carcinogenic. But Lavinia developed cancer of the bone and we were unable to save her.

My own brush with cancer was quickly dealt with, and the tumour was successfully removed. Since then I have carefully regulated the medication and reduced the dosage. I believe it is easier than we thought to switch on the telomerase gene. It is no great effort to persuade the chromosomes to repair their telomeres. They only need a nudge.

So MM told you without asking me. He thinks he knows

better. He thinks he knows me better than I know myself. Is there anything more irritating than that?

I can't help noticing that time has taken its toll on MM. One way or another he has already become diluted. Gradually he has developed a paunch, his hair is quite grey, and the skin on his neck is slackening. When we talk, I am aware that I am taller than him. And I no longer try to hide it.

Still, he made another appeal. I well knew that, behind my back, he had contacted the *Guardian* newspaper, and set a journalist on my trail. However, I decided not to mention this. And MM did not mention it either. Perhaps he was ashamed.

He said, 'Dr Victor Zimmerman.'

'Yes?'

I looked at him with surprise, but affectionately. I waited for him to continue.

'May I ask,' MM said, 'what exactly you think you are doing?'

Over the years MM's English has improved a lot. I must say I regret the eccentric phraseology of his youth. There is hardly anything left of the Russian wildness his speech used to have, hardly a trace of the brilliant alien I used to love, the impetuous being who came to us from Moscow trailing a host of previous lives.

'In case you didn't know,' I said, 'I am trying out a new drug.'

'Yes. And how is it affecting you?'

'What do you think?'

I stood before him, undeniably in fine fettle, embarrassingly healthy. The fact is, I was looking far better than him. I searched for his bright blue eyes, but what I saw was milky, like the eyes of a fish on a slab.

'It is clear,' he said, 'that you are physically well. But what is happening inside your head?'

'I have no idea what you are referring to.'

'To put it crudely, to oversimplify perhaps – I am thinking of mirror neurons.'

'Mirror neurons again.'

'Yes – those brain cells that reflect the feelings of other people. What makes us human, in a way. So we can understand others, sympathise, feel connected. Et cetera.'

'MM,' I said. 'You are a fine scientist. You know I have always respected you. But you don't have to tell me about mirror neurons. I know as much about them as you do.'

'Of course,' he replied. 'No one yet knows the precise function of mirror neurons. I speak of them as a symbol of something else. That part of us which is not entirely egocentric.'

He stared at me. Was he trying to look threatening? I found this faintly amusing.

I remembered his enthusiastic embrace of an expression I myself had suggested: the self-transcending drive. But now this expression seemed to me a little pompous, a little simplistic.

'Victor,' he said. 'You have always been a good person. Understanding and kind. You and I have discussed many things, and seen eye to eye. But now you are rushing away, on a different track.'

I have to say, that nowadays the word 'good', in relation to a person, gives me the creeps. MM himself was what you call a 'good person', though infuriating.

'What makes you say that?'

MM did not answer directly.

He said, 'There is a simple solution. Publish. Open the debate.'

'And what would that do?'

'It will check you. It will make you think. You will no longer be alone. You will share.'

MM seemed sincere. But was he really being honest? Did he really believe so fervently in 'sharing'?

'All right,' I said. 'I have already decided to do so. I will write to the *Lancet*. Or would *Genome* be better?'

'Whichever,' he replied. 'Or both.'

'Yes, both. All right.'

Briefly, a memory flashed through me: I saw the boy I once

was, exploring the disused storeroom in our house in Camden Town, and finding there the biology textbook which had belonged to Andres Ferreira.

'Can I trust you?'

'Of course.'

MM took a deep breath. He said, 'Well done, Victory.' It was a long time, I thought, since he had called me Victory. 'At last, you are ready. I assure you, you have nothing to hide.'

♦♦

I collected the relevant papers from the lab, the details of our progress, our trials and errors, and took them to the house in Castir.

I sat down in my study and began to put them in order.

Behind me was the little fridge keeping the magic inhalers at just the right temperature. Through the window undulating hills stretched to the horizon, with their geometric patterns of olive trees. The glow of evening filled the sky, a mauve light rose from the earth like a mantle.

It was high summer, already the end of July. The bougainvillea in our garden was almost over, and little green knobs were forming on the walnut trees.

I sat back in my chair. On the computer I opened a new document and gazed at the empty screen. Eventually I wrote: 'I am one of those lucky enough to have work which fascinates him.'

I heard an owl cry. I became aware of solitude, of self-containment. I felt the strong beating of my heart. Softly I imitated the call of the owl. I had learnt to do this on the mountainside. Sometimes a whole horde of owls would answer me, and once a bird flew right over me in the dark, flapping its heavy wings.

Lucy's voice came from downstairs: 'Victor, it's dinner time, could you lay the table?' Obediently I put the papers away and switched off the computer. I repeated my own name: Victor ...

was I Victor? I walked slowly down the stairs, knowing exactly which would creak and which wouldn't. I repeated to myself: Victor, could you lay the table?

I paused on the last step. Through the kitchen door I saw Lucy, carrying a pot to the table, the tendons standing out on her thin arms. Her hair was held back in a greying bun. I watched her small pianist's hands as she lowered the pot onto a mat.

I became aware of a decision. A decision rose from the depths.

I couldn't do it. Something overwhelming was preventing me. I couldn't write to *Genome*, or any other magazine. To do so would be a denial, a betrayal of myself. Above all, I had to respect my deepest desire; what else mattered? When I realised this, a great weight flew from my shoulders; and in an instant I became free.

I sighed with relief.

I would write nothing. I would disclose no more secrets.

I would be the only one.

◆◆

During dinner Lucy and I kept up a light, friendly conversation. Over dessert, a delicate *fondant au chocolat* with chestnut filling, we relaxed. I had to curb my appetite; sometimes I seem to eat faster than other people.

You said, 'Your hair's black again.'

I replied, trying to be funny, 'My hairdresser has never seen anything like it.'

You laughed.

I continued, 'Yes, that's the big surprise about the treatment. It doesn't just prolong life. It actually rejuvenates! We weren't expecting that. But otherwise,' I smiled, 'it wouldn't be any use. Who'd want to go on for ever if you just got more decrepit?'

You said, 'When I first met you, you had thick black hair and it was curly. Now it's thick, and black – but it's straight.'

I said, 'Yes, I've noticed that. Anything else?'

You got up and fetched a photo. I knew the picture well; it was kept on the hall table. There was a youngish Victor, sitting on a low wall in bright sunlight. Behind him Lake Como in Italy sparkled into the distance. I remembered the moment clearly. Victor was smiling happily at the camera. He was wearing a linen jacket, a blue open shirt, his hands were folded in his lap.

'Come,' you said, taking my hand and leading me into the room with the piano. I thought perhaps you were going to play some soulful music, to remind me of the old days. Instead you led me to a mirror.

'Smile,' you said.

I watched as my lips drew apart. My hair bounced above my forehead and fell over my ears.

'Smile some more,' you said.

I tried. Of course it was impossible to reproduce Victor's glowing expression as he sat on the wall in Como. You had to have a reason for it. But I tried. Behind me you held the photograph beside my face. I saw both in the mirror. There wasn't much difference, I thought. My eyebrows had grown thicker, and the nose perhaps softer. My brow had advanced into a ridge, making the eyes more deep set. This was an improvement; I had always found Victor's eyes a little flat. The line of the jaw was just as sharp as in the picture, with no double chin. My cheeks looked plumper than before, if anything more youthful. My teeth, as far as I could see, looked fine and had not changed.

But there was something new, in the mirror version: on my upper lip, a little to the right, was a black mole. When I smiled the new mole stretched and became more visible. It looked as if a drop of something sticky was about to roll into my mouth. From the collar of my shirt tufts of hair sprouted and crept up round my neck – another development. In the photo Victor's neck was hairless.

'You see?' you said.

'What?'

'Your smile's changed.'

I took a deep breath. This was a stupid comment. All the same, to please you, I tried again. I closed my eyes and tried to imagine you in the old days. I remembered walking hand in hand beside Lake Como. But then I was in love! I almost said. I tried to smile simply, innocently, and opened my eyes. Now the smile stretched right across my face, exposing fine white teeth, like the young man sitting on the wall in Como. It was perfect in its way.

I said, 'In the course of the years almost every cell in the body is replaced a number of times. Flesh dies and is reborn. None of this,' I said, touching my face, 'no bit of it is exactly the same as it was when that photograph was taken. It is similar but not identical.'

'My darling,' you said.

Now I hadn't heard these words for quite a long time. It was almost a whisper. And that whisper, your whisper, moved me all over again. 'My darling.' I found myself smiling – this time it was a real smile. I glanced in the mirror, sure I would see it. But I didn't. It was still the new smile. But what was wrong with that? The skin looked healthy, the lips full and curved. Yet there was something odd, I could see it myself, a kind of polish, a veneer, as if the whole face had been lightly varnished. Or was it the new mole on the lip that gave this impression, the glistening beauty spot?

'There are thousands of muscles in the face,' I began, turning back.

You were still looking at me with love, your eyes were shining. I felt like a swimmer when the sea recedes, drawn out by a strong tide. All this time we had gone on as before, the rhythm had hardly changed, making love, discussing your concerts, my work, walking together in Castir. And yet you were there on the shore and I was far out.

I made an extraordinary decision: for Lucy, I would give up telo.

I took you in my arms and covered you with kisses. 'I'm coming back,' I murmured.

I told you the full story of telo. I led you to the sofa, took your hands in mine, and explained it all. I told you about telomeres, the repeated chemical bases at the ends of chromosomes that keep them intact. I described our research into telomerase. I explained why it is that evolution has not bothered much with telomerase, leaving the body, after the reproductive age, to grow fragile and decay.

I said, 'We are like a great violinist whose instrument turns to dust in his hands, and is irreplaceable.'

You replied, almost laughing: 'But violins improve with age!'

I said, 'Yes – and so can we. For this process is not inevitable. It is not irreversible. The gene for telomerase is present in every cell in the body. It is there, dormant, patient, waiting for the signal. And we have discovered how to send the signal.'

When I had finished you looked up at me and said, 'And now you intend to give it all up?'

I nodded. 'I'll have to phase it out gradually. Unless … unless you'd like to try it too.'

You answered immediately. 'Me? No, I don't think so, Victor.'

'All right,' I said. 'But think about it. Don't put it out of your mind.'

You found the whole thing frightening. Of course, I understood. It was the normal human reaction. But that would change, gradually, with familiarity. Gene therapy would become accepted, standard, just another branch of medicine. One day no one would be able to resist telomerase. To do so would be a form of suicide. It would be saying no to life.

'What will you do with them?' you asked. 'The inhalers?'

'Oh, that hardly matters. Take them back to the lab, I expect.'

I smiled at you, wondering whether the varnish, or whatever it was that had suddenly seemed repellent, was gone from my face. I almost got up to have a look in the mirror. But I began to have an odd feeling; a hole was opening up, and something inside was leaking away, emptying me. I stood up and did a funny little dance, to make light of the whole thing. But the leaking feeling persisted. I smiled lovingly at you; and with the tip of my tongue examined the shiny black mole on my upper lip. But my guts were churning, my body was in revolt.

'Yes, my darling,' I said. 'Lock it away in the lab!'

You went on: 'Victor, you know how I have always loved – what shall I call it? – your spirit, your sense of adventure … you drew me out of my musical cocoon, you showed me how to live.'

I put in: 'I never wanted to take you away from music. On the contrary. You know how much I love music and admire your playing.'

Victor, in the past, was quite bowled over by your playing; he could spend hours in his study listening to you practise through the floorboards.

Surprising, isn't it? I said to myself – to the two of us, the two Victors; surprising how much we have changed.

◆◆

Now you mentioned the most terrible period in your life. After our baby son's death your hands turned to wood and for a long time you could not touch the piano. When you started again, hesitantly, like a beginner, there was some music, especially Schubert, that you could not bear to play. It was too heartbreaking.

You sat stiffly on the sofa beside me and began to cry. I took you in my arms. I felt the thinness of your body, your collarbones brittle like a bird so that if I pressed too hard I was afraid you might crack and shatter into pieces. You were small, you had always been small, but in the old days there was a solidness about you, a softness from top to toe, except for your hands which were strong and sinewy. But now I felt I could lift you in my arms and hardly notice the weight. You were bony and thin, the veins stood out on your arms, and this was not just due to age. In your thinness as I held you I felt a kind of mental disorder, a sense of desolation. You were really sobbing in my arms, and sometimes you buried your head in my shoulder and at other moments tried to pull away. You made your hand into a fist and your knuckles turned white.

Apart from the time around our baby's death I had never seen Lucy crying very much. If she was angry with me she tended to withdraw, to switch off, and even after I apologised for something I might or might not have done, it took her a long time to come round. I would apologise, humiliate myself, even if, really, I had done nothing wrong. Because I couldn't bear her coldness; it felt as if I was being condemned to outer darkness. Sometimes, in the middle of a sulk, she would go off and play the piano and then I was surprised to hear that she seemed to get into her work without difficulty. Afterwards I thought the music would have cured her but as soon as she saw me she became just as cold as before.

Now, as you can imagine, I am no longer afraid of 'outer darkness'!

In any case, Lucy's sulkiness went away long ago, and I'm not sure why I remembered it that day when I promised to give up telo and held her sobbing in my arms. Now it was she who seemed to be apologising and asking again and again if I understood. And I replied that I did, as I have always done; on one of our first meetings you said that I was 'one of those people who understand everything'. And that was one of the most important things, perhaps the thing above all that you liked me for. Empathy has always been one of my strongest points, it comes you know from my 'feminine' side, which was well balanced with the masculine, etc., etc.

I understand, my darling, I whispered, stroking your hair with my powerful hands. I gave you a loving, heartfelt smile, although aware that it maybe still didn't look like the old one. And I couldn't do anything about the new mole on my upper lip, which added its own touch of darkness. It was terrible to see you so distraught. I let you cry in my arms, rocking you gently.

For she was Lucy, the love of my life.

I was, however, at the same time thinking about the woman

who ran the grocery store in the village of Castir. Her name was Maria, she was a grandmother, though still young, and she knew everything that happened in the village. I was thinking that Maria was bound to know of someone who had a room to let. And in this room I could keep my little locked fridge with the sealed bottles and plastic inhalers. It should not be too difficult to organise. Because otherwise I would have to keep it in the lab and make sure I was in London every time I needed a dose. And I didn't want to do this because I wanted to spend more time in Castir.

But wasn't I going to give it up?

There was also the problem of MM. How on earth could I keep that mad Russian quiet? I began to imagine all sorts of chemical combinations. It became a pastime to dream up ever more subtle varieties of poison; perhaps his laboratory coat could become impregnated. I could hardly stop thinking about this and brought all my scientific knowledge to bear. I would not try to kill him, but gradually, over a long period, impair his nervous system. In this way his brilliant mind would deteriorate and he would leave me alone. There was of course a simpler old-fashioned solution – the leaking stove pipe in the bedroom. But that was clumsy.

Meanwhile my dear Lucy was crying her heart out. I stroked her gently and uttered calming words. I couldn't help noticing how hairy my hands had become. Of course I would give up telo, I told her, and all would return to normal. Then we would love each other as before and grow old serenely in each other's arms.

If I did give up, would my body rapidly deteriorate and suddenly become the body of a seventy-year-old? It was an interesting question. Actually I think not; it is more likely the deterioration would begin where I left off.

But what *was* my body's age, now, at this moment, as Lucy wept beside me on the sofa? I really was ageless, in a way no one had ever been before, and in fact getting steadily younger, while the days and months sped on into the future as usual. This was such an intoxicating thought, though one that had often occurred to me before, that I laughed out loud; and Lucy, seeing me so merry, laughed too. She dried her tears on her sleeve, and we both laughed hard, for quite a long time, as people sometimes do after coming through a terrible experience together.

I was becoming good at keeping opposite things in my head at the same time. For Lucy's sake I might well give up telo and we would grow old happily together, as if nothing had happened; yet at the same time I was wondering how to find a room in the village to keep my medication and continue to administer the fortnightly doses.

This was the sort of duplicity, of course, that an 'addict' is very good at; he is very good, I mean, at limiting his duplicity to one particular area and being honest in others.

And I have always been honest, wherever possible. Oh, he always considers others, people said. I had what is called compassion – an interesting state of mind which does not, at the time, when you have it, seem fake.

Could I have my cake and eat it?

I gazed gently at Lucy and saw a person in the grip of strong emotions; a person painfully dependent on others. She was in my power; a word from me could make her happy or condemn her to misery. But I myself felt no such thing; who could make any difference to me?

Nevertheless, I do not want to lose entirely the person I was before, dear old Victor. Nor the things that mattered to him so much – music, for example … music which has the power to awaken deep feeling, to re-awaken … is that what it does? Mind you, it is at the same time a well-documented fact that some of the worst monsters in history were music lovers; some of those who only cared about their personal gratification were apparently moved by music.

And how is such a thing possible? There is some obscure sense that I can somehow understand this, now that I myself have become … But I can't help feeling that the emotions I once experienced while listening to music were a kind of – well, to tell the truth, I'm not sure what they were. I was going to say 'a kind of sham', but that would be unfair. It's just that the old Victor, with all his great emotions, seems to me a rather comic figure.

Anyway, I went on comforting Lucy, even though I was, at the same time, planning to keep the medicine in a rented room in the village and go on rejuvenating – while at the same time managing not to let it show, for it would perhaps be possible (and even amusing) to *pretend* to be decrepit, to become apparently more and more decrepit, as Lucy herself is bound to do (and is already doing).

Meanwhile she was crying and laughing and hanging on to me on the sofa, and there was something dogged about the way she was doing it, something absolutely determined not to give up. I found this faintly unappealing. The sofa itself, on which we were bouncing from side to side, caught my attention and I remembered that it was the same old sofa that my parents had in our house in Camden Town when I was a child. It was different now, rather as I was, firm and neatly upholstered in green velvet; but in those days its brown leather covering was peeling so badly that as a boy I used to enjoy pulling off small strips and digging my fingers into the woolly stuff beneath.

Lucy sighed and nuzzled against my neck; and pressed her fingers into my hair, pulling it this way and that, as if trying to twist it back into the curls she apparently so loved in the old days.

It was a kind of massage, and I closed my eyes. The feel of Lucy's fingers against my scalp was stimulating.

I was filled with all sorts of memories from the past.

◆◆

How was it, I used to wonder, that my mother married my father?

As Lucy played with my hair, I saw my mother again; vivid

and glamorous as she was, even while doing the vacuum cleaning or ironing her nurse's uniform. She had a luminous grace,
entirely unselfconscious. She stood out from others like a rose
that stands alone in a disordered garden.

My father, on the other hand, was quite different. When he
spoke, he expected people not to listen. He had a habit of stopping in the middle of his sentences, and then starting again from
the beginning – even if people were, in fact, listening. And then
sometimes he did it again.

My 'father': a kindly, meticulous man, with whom I felt
nothing in common. And nor, I think, did my mother.

She told me once, when I was a teenager: I married him
because of a picture. As a young man my father's hobby was
painting. But, in my lifetime, I never saw him with a pencil or
brush in his hand.

'I married him,' she said, 'because of that!'

Laughing she pointed at a picture on the wall of our sitting
room in Camden Town; a picture I knew so well I had hardly
even noticed it.

But I was looking at it now. For there it was, in Castir,
hanging in front of me, a few feet from the sofa on which we
were having our drama, Lucy and I, our 'reconciliation'; the
picture my father once painted.

The picture looks Indian, or Middle-Eastern. A young man
with a pale face is riding an elephant. The man and his elephant
move carefully through a rocky landscape. He wears flowing
robes and sits on a decorated seat; on his head is a golden head-
dress with two bobbing feathers, one black, one blue.

'And what,' asked my mother, 'what is he thinking about, the
peaceful man on the elephant?'

I looked at her, wondering what she meant. There were
perhaps clues in the landscape, a dry solitary place; in the background was a bank on which clumps of flowers grew, and a
small twisted tree. But I saw no way of telling what the man was
thinking about.

'The answer,' my mother said, 'is in the body of the elephant.'

I looked carefully. The elephant's body was not grey but painted in various colours and patterns. I had taken this as decoration, a kind of ceremonial cloth. But in fact the elephant's skin itself was painted all over with tiny scenes – there were human figures and animals in strange positions, reaching up or down, stretching out or curled into balls, each quite separate, yet the scenes over-lapped, on the body, the head, the trunk, the tusks, and the legs right down to the four square feet with stubby pinkish toenails. And there were abstract shapes too, representing nothing clear, indeterminate forms in green, mauve, red and other colours.

I was surprised that my father could have dreamt up a thing like that.

'You see?' she said. 'He's got all that on his mind, the young man in the picture. That's what he's thinking about.'

But what exactly? Nothing could be less clear.

I watched my mother; her eyes were bright, her teeth glisten-ing, her hair fell in harmonious curves around her chin. I looked at her eyes, shining like jewels, and wondered if all minds, once you got past the bright windows, were as strange as that of the elephant rider in the picture. And he, the young man, had a quiet, tranquil face; could his mind be full of such meaningless, amorphous shapes? As for myself, my own thoughts seemed to be clear and direct, I knew very well what I was thinking at any moment.

But as I looked at my mother, and at the picture, and at her again, I thought that perhaps there was something else, in the faint lines on her brow, in the shadows within her pupils, something I could not grasp. I looked at her curiously. Perhaps I didn't know her as well as I thought. Perhaps nothing was quite what it seemed, perhaps what I saw in her limpid face was just the foam on the waves, the spray from the deep, and beyond lay vague, indescribable monsters. I remembered the photo of the giant squid, which I had torn from the *National Geographic*. And the bright sunlit seas on the page before.

We looked at the picture in silence, my mother and I. The picture of the young man in flowing robes, riding the elephant.

It was as if we were letting go, allowing the hidden monsters to come up for air.

I said to Lucy, 'Look. My father painted that.'

Lucy turned and looked at it, surprised as if like little Victor she had hardly noticed it before. She even got off the sofa and went to inspect the painting close up. I watched her from behind. Her skirt was rather short and her legs still shapely. Below her left knee was a small cluster of veins, quite normal for someone of her age.

She turned back and said how beautiful it was. Then she went into the kitchen and fetched a bottle of port, to celebrate our reconciliation. I was pleased to see her happy.

Meanwhile I began considering how best to remove the fridge and its contents to their new destination. It would be necessary to do this when Lucy was away from the house. She was due to go on another concert tour, in a few weeks' time. But it would be a good idea to get rid of the fridge as soon as possible, or she might not believe in my renunciation.

It would be foolish, I realised, to rent a room in Castir; I would go to the neighbouring village. I began imagining possible locations. The new room need not be big, but it must have a separate entrance and a door with a lock. It might be at the top of the village where there were some old houses with views directly onto the mountain. I would put in a comfortable armchair facing the window. And, I thought, I would hang the painting there, of the man with the elephant.

Lucy came in with the port. We raised our glasses and drank to the future. At the same time I visualised my new room with growing excitement.

I liked the idea of an empty space, simple, with wooden floorboards, a fireplace, and perhaps some pretty tiles, as in many of the houses in Castir. I could picture myself there, in the evening light, unlocking the fridge, taking out an inhaler, settling myself in the armchair, watching the mountain.

I asked Lucy when her concerts were, when she was going to Germany. On the wall before us I saw the young man on the elephant, and they seemed to move slowly forward, the man leaning back as the elephant stepped down among the rocks. On the beast's body the images shifted and became elastic with the movement of his skin.

◆◆

When her dementia began, my mother came out with funny things, which took me by surprise. I laughed, and she laughed too, without knowing why.

One morning, sitting in her little garden: 'You know I'm so worried about my poor pigeons. Yesterday they killed two cats. And all that was left was feathers.'

To become a burden was always her nightmare. Her dementia worsened and she could no longer walk. Her head slumped forward and she found it harder and harder to feed herself. As a nurse she had seen people live like this, helpless, for many years.

One day she came out of her trance and said, 'You know I saw Laura yesterday.'

'Did you?'

'Yes, she was wearing such a pretty skirt.'

'Was she? But you know, Laura died some years ago.'

'Really?' she replied, turning to me. 'Well, she didn't *look* dead.'

She smiled sweetly, her words blew away and she was silent again, as if she had said nothing at all. And I realised that there wasn't much difference for her between the living and the dead, she could look all day immobile in her chair at the people outside her window, and they were like moving dots on a screen; for she was already elsewhere.

I said to Lucy, 'Actually, as far as that painting is concerned, my father deceived my mother. She took it for an original work and was so impressed that she fell in love with him. He didn't tell her at first, and I can understand that. But later, once they were married, he confessed: I copied it from a Persian miniature. It was just a copy! Though well painted, don't you think?'

Lucy nodded. But she was not much interested in these reminiscences. Her thoughts were on us, the happiness we had known together, and would perhaps know once more.

She filled my glass and we drank again to the future. Like an engulfing cloud I felt her joy; with hesitant, disordered steps we were walking towards each other.

But I was at the same time in another place – my new room in the next village. And now I saw it differently: not a bare functional space like a doctor's surgery, but a lair, a den of comfort, with chairs, cushions, tables, interesting objects, a darkish room with low lamps, bookcases, rugs, a warm enveloping place with a smell of old leather, soft fabrics, the fridge itself concealed by a hanging brocade! Yes, I saw the room like this, a haven – where all the sweetest things in the world were gathered; a love nest. I open the door, stand on the threshold, am drawn in, welcomed, embraced; just as, long ago, I sat on the low wall by the lake in Como and Lucy stood in front of me; her blue-black blouse rose and fell, I knew she was mine, in her dark eyes I saw something wild, and I believed there was nothing more I could need or desire.

Yes, that is how it was. But now, instead of L, there was telo.

We went to bed and fell straightaway into an intoxicated sleep.

After a few hours I woke. We were lying on our sides, fitting snugly together, like two spoons, as we used to say. We always said how well we fitted, neither of us too big, our shapes matching.

Through the open window I heard the crickets sing. They sang like a surrounding army, triumphant. For a while I listened to the crickets and Lucy's breathing. For a little while I basked in the sadness of it all, and the beauty, two lovers trying for a moment to stop the world. It was as if I had forgotten; I allowed myself a moment of nostalgia, a breath from the past.

But I was smiling; my head was clear, I was refreshed, how well I was, how strong, how free!

I watched as dawn broke. I closed my eyes again and immediately began dreaming. It was an old dream, a dream I recognised even while I was dreaming it: I'm a boy in our house in Camden Town. I open a hidden door in the wall and find myself in another part of the house, a series of large rooms leading from one to the next. I half recognised the rooms, as if I'd known them once, and thought: so now I know how to get here! The rooms were huge, filled with light; there were high windows, chandeliers, and in one a four-poster bed. Log fires were burning in fireplaces so large I could walk into them. I tiptoe from one room to another, amazed by the stillness and evening sunlight falling in shafts onto wooden floors. I thought: how extraordinary that these rooms have always been here, and I had quite forgotten about them.

23

I woke again, got out of bed and dressed. Lucy was still asleep; I kissed her on the forehead and left the house. These days I don't seem to need much sleep. And I don't like to miss the early morning.

I went back up the hill, to the camper van. The Cayman's door closed behind me with a satisfying click. For four days and nights I stayed there, happy in my solitude. I texted Lucy to let her know I was fine.

There was a hint of damp in the late summer air. The days were drawing in.

Several times I went for a swim in the river. Underwater swimming is my joy; to look down, eyes open, through clear water, at the rocks, grasses and darting fish below. To emerge gleaming onto a boulder, to feel my hair wet and slicked back, to see the glassy drops on my skin. Glorious youth.

Then it was time for my fortnightly dose.

As the time approaches, I begin to feel restless. Even if I lost count of the days, my inner clock never would.

Rather stupidly, I still keep telo in the house – I haven't yet sorted out another place. I could keep it in the Cayman, but I don't trust the electricity supply. The fridge temperature might not be stable.

In a drawer in the van I keep a small collection of curiosities. Dried flowers, a butterfly wing, and a mechanical device for lopping off the top of boiled eggs. That sort of thing. My cabinet of curiosities. From here I selected a small present for Lucy.

I came down from the Cayman to the house. Lucy was practising the piano in the room above my study and I didn't think she would hear me.

I took my medication; and relaxed in the armchair by the window. As usual I dozed off for a few minutes. Then I went into the room where Lucy was playing, and sat on the sofa. I did not want to interrupt her.

Lucy had told me that I was her best listener, and she never felt nervous when she played for me. Sometimes, she said, in a public concert she imagined that she was playing for me alone, even when I was not in the audience.

Now she glanced at me without stopping, and I could see she was pleased I was there. I listened quietly. She was playing Schumann's 'Fantasie Op. 17', and the heaving, restless music filled the room.

In the middle of the first movement, at an intense moment, she stopped.

'Go on,' I said.

'But you're not listening.'

'Of course I'm listening.'

She got up from the piano and took a step towards me. I sat without moving and smiled at her.

'What's wrong?' I said. 'You look at me strangely. But I'm still the same person – can't you see that? It's still me.'

Was there a hint of despair in my voice? I do not think so. On the contrary, I felt triumphant. Yes, I sat there triumphantly. How young and attractive I must look, I thought, my skin smooth, my hair black and shiny. I wore jeans and a green T-shirt printed with the names of cities: LONDON, COPENHAGEN, BERLIN.

'Music doesn't mean much to you any more, does it?' she said.

I raised my eyebrows. 'What do you mean?'

'It's just noise to you now, isn't it?'

I said, 'Lucy, as a scientist, a researcher, I've been trying out something new and unexpected. I have a responsibility to try it on myself first. That's all. And soon I shall stop. All that I was before, the Victor that you've always known, is still there. How could he disappear? Please go on, darling.'

I heard my own voice; it was just the same – easy, fluent, reassuring.

Lucy sat down at the piano, closed her eyes and began again. I watched her closely. This time she got to the end of the piece.

I clapped. 'Marvellous,' I said.

She seemed surprised. 'Usually you don't clap,' she said, 'when I play just for you.'

This annoyed me slightly. Still, I went over to the piano and kissed her on the cheek. 'I've got a present for you,' I said.

I took it from my pocket and gave it to her. She held it under the piano lamp.

'What is it?' she asked. 'A piece of leather? It stinks of something – I'm not sure what.'

'It's a shoe,' I said. 'It's part of the oldest shoe ever found. Look, you can even see the imprint of a big toe.'

'A shoe?'

'Yes – over 5,000 years old. It was found in a cave in Armenia. Isn't that wonderful?' I took the little piece of leather from her, and held it to my nose. 'The smell of the past. Think of it! A man, 5,000 years ago, wearing a shoe, just like us. And here it is now, in our hands.'

She suddenly clutched at me, and the shoe fell to the floor.

'Careful,' I said. 'It's fragile.'

I picked it up and beamed at her.

'You appreciate these things,' I said.

I saw her looking down at my feet. They were bare, in sandals. My toes twitched. I knew what was going through her head; it was easy to read her mind.

Oh Victor, she was thinking. How you loved to take off your shoes, to walk barefoot in the park! Do you remember those long walks on the mountainside – when we would stop and listen for birds, and marvel at everything, rocks, leaves, insects, trees, and come home at last together with tired and aching limbs?

'It was stuffed with grass,' I said. 'To preserve the shape. Can you imagine bothering with that, in a cave?'

I wanted to say more; but something odd happened. My mouth was open, but no sound came out. It was as if I was frozen. I tried to blink; but my eyelids would not move.

Lucy seized my hand.

Then it was over. I breathed out, and my shoulders dropped. I was mobile again.

'I don't expect it to mean as much to you,' I said, withdrawing my hand. 'But still – keep it. I've got another piece.'

'Keep what?'

'The shoe.'

The freezing spasm was over so quickly I'm not sure it really happened. To this day I'm not sure; it might have been my imagination.

In any case there was clearly nothing wrong with me. I stood before Lucy straight and tall, solid, handsome, my skin burnished, perhaps a little darker than before. But I didn't quite know what to say. And nor, apparently, did she. Suddenly, for the first time, we had nothing to say to each other. It was almost embarrassing, as if we were strangers unable to make conversation.

'Thank you,' she said at last. 'I'll certainly keep it.'

'It's a memento,' I replied.

'A memento – of what?'

I couldn't exactly say: of us, of our love. So I said nothing.

She stepped backwards, and knocked against the piano. Once again the shoe fell to the floor. But she quickly picked it up and held it against her cheek. She wanted to speak, I could see. I smiled encouragingly.

'Victor,' she began.

'Yes?'

'Is it really you – my husband? The man I have always admired?'

'Of course,' I replied. 'Touch me.' I took her hand and guided it to my face.

But she pulled away.

'Oh dear,' I said. 'I am not a dummy, you know.'

'But you are not …'

'Not what?'

'Not quite …'

'Not quite what?'

'Not quite the Victor I have loved …' she got it out at last. 'No,' she went on, rather heartlessly. 'You have become a kind of – impostor.'

An impostor? I looked into Lucy's black eyes. And I saw myself reflected there. What I saw was not exactly an impostor; no – it was a double. A double! I had turned into a double of myself. I was a double of the old Victor; and this double was, in fact, now the 'real me'.

This was an interesting thought, but nonsense, of course.

'Don't be stupid,' I said.

She shook her head. 'I'm not being stupid.'

'I'll leave then,' I said. 'If that's what you'd like.'

And the fact was: I too wanted to leave.

'Is the Cayman comfortable?'

'Oh yes,' I nodded. 'Come and see one day. Bye bye. Keep the shoe safe.' I smiled at her cruelly. Odd, the thought crossed my mind, the different ways one can smile.

'Time for the impostor to get back,' I said.

24

Autumn has come again. In the mornings the Cayman is veiled in mist, which sometimes takes all day to clear. The mountainside no longer smells of wild herbs, but of fungus and earth and mould. I like this smell. The months pass so quickly, I have long ago stopped counting them. But I am sensitive to the changing seasons; they are my time marker.

I sit in the van in the evening, pondering the problem of MM. His body is weakening rapidly, but his mind is still acute.

In the house we have a wood-burning stove and a long flue which goes up through the spare bedroom. The top joint is not secure. If you tap it, at just the right place, you get a gap. Dangerous, as carbon monoxide could seep out. If the bedroom window is closed –

Somebody was knocking at the door of the Cruiser.

I took the torch and went outside. It was quite windy. A youngish man stood beside the van. He was wearing a padded jacket with the logo North Face, and an open shirt. On his feet were trainers, probably expensive, but now scuffed and dirty. A canvas bag hung from his shoulder.

'Can I help you?' I said.

'Please excuse me,' he replied. 'I called at your house in the village, and was told I might find you here.' He spoke in English, with only a slight foreign accent.

'Well done,' I said. 'It's a hard walk up here. And tricky, in the dark.'

'I am tough,' the man replied. 'And I have come a long way to see you.'

I suspected the truth immediately. To speed things up, I took the initiative.

'You are a journalist?' I enquired.

'That is correct. I work for *Le Monde*, in Paris. We are most interested in your work.'

Now I understood his accent; he was French.

'I must apologise,' the man went on, 'for bothering you. This is a strange place to meet. But would you mind if we did a short interview?'

'Of course not,' I said. 'I am happy to talk to you.'

I shone the torch into his face. He wore a peaked cap, and under it I saw a pair of dark cunning eyes, set rather close. His nose was bulbous, with blue veins visible around the base. The skin of his cheeks was blotchy.

Probably he had been drinking in the village, before making the climb to my hideaway.

'I'll get a bottle of wine,' I said. 'Then we can have a drink together. Would you like that?'

'With pleasure.'

'Please come inside.'

I led him in, poured us both a glass of red wine, and we sat down. It was, I must say, a cosy scene; the oil lamp gave off an old-fashioned glow, casting ghostlike shadows on the walls, while outside the wind whined and whistled round the corners of the Cayman.

'May I ask,' I began, 'who contacted your newspaper? Who told you, I mean, about me?'

'Oh, I'm sure you understand – I can't reveal my sources.'

'Of course.' I smiled knowingly. 'What is it you wanted to talk to me about?'

The man cleared his throat. 'Would you mind,' he asked, 'if I record our conversation?'

'Not at all.'

He took a small digital recorder from his bag and laid it on the table.

'You know,' he said, 'we at *Le Monde* have always followed your work. You are a hero to us, and of course to many others. All the people you have helped over the years! And now this experiment.'

How much did he know, I wondered. And who had told him?

'What experiment are you referring to?'

'Oh, you know – the anti-ageing drug. Is it true that you are trying out something of this sort? On yourself?'

'You are well informed. Before a drug becomes commercially available, we have to make sure it is safe. It is a matter of principle – to try it on ourselves.'

'How brave. And what are the results, so far?'

I smiled. 'Oh, fairly positive. I have not experienced any negative side effects. Nothing major.'

'That is tremendously exciting. And is the drug working as expected?'

I made a non-committal expression, and shrugged my shoulders.

'I suppose you have regular check-ups?'

'Yes indeed.'

'Of course, as a science journalist, I am hoping to write an article.' The man took a deep breath. 'But, in addition, I have a personal interest in your experiment.'

'Is that so? But, in fact, all of us have a personal interest.'

'Naturally. But for me it has a particular ring. Please forgive me. It is so kind to grant me an interview.'

'I am open to enquiries.'

'It was an effort to find you! But now that I am here, in your lair ...'

'Please go on.'

'Well ... the fact is, there was a time when my life meant nothing to me. I fell into a depression. I had completely lost – the taste of things.'

'I understand.'

'One night ... I took too many sleeping pills.'

'Oh dear. It is easy to be tempted by oblivion.'

The man nodded.

'It is true,' I said, 'that life can be overwhelming. So many worries. So many contradictions. Too complicated.'

'Yes, the human dilemma. All those brain cells ...' The man sighed. 'It was too much for me.'

'But you survived.'

'I did, as you can see.' He paused. 'And then, one day I went to Italy for a holiday.'

'A good choice.'

'I visited the Greek temples at Paestum. South of Naples. Have you been there?'

I shook my head.

'You should. They are magnificent.'

'I have heard of them.'

'It was a low point in my life. But while I was walking there, in Paestum ... I suddenly saw the beauty of everything around me – the ancient temples, still rising high, the ruined columns, and the wild flowers. It was a kind of revelation. I decided, then and there, to pull myself together. I didn't want to die, after all.'

'A joyful discovery.'

'I realised that I didn't want to throw away my life. It was far too precious. It wasn't rubbish, after all.'

'Life is the greatest gift we have.' This was a cliché, of course. But it was what the man expected.

'And yet, despite the beauty,' he went on, 'despite my relief – I found Italy sad. All that history, and yet the people who created it were so long dead. I saw that life was just – how do you say – a flash in the pan. Almost gone before it starts.'

'Your English is very good,' I said. 'A flash in the pan. Excellent expression.'

'Yet – how I wanted to live!'

The man was silent. He looked sadly down at his shoes. It was almost as if we were two old friends sharing confidences. But I had seen his sharp fox-like eyes. And on the table a little red light shone on the recording machine.

I said, 'We walk in darkness. And then, sometimes, an opportunity comes.'

'Yes. And you are in the forefront of us all. We follow you with true admiration.'

Somehow, and quickly, I would dispose of him. I was not sure how. But I would do it.

'I am just a scientist,' I said. 'Like so many others.'

Now the man looked up at me. His eyes were bleary. A single glass of wine had been enough to push him over the limit. Unless he was pretending.

'And what you have discovered now,' he went on, slightly slurring his words, 'gives us all hope.'

'Yes,' I said. 'The time has come.'

'For what exactly?'

It hardly mattered now. I would let go. I would impress him.

'At home,' I said, 'I have a fridge full of little inhalers, my own invention. Like for asthmatics. They work perfectly. Every day I grow younger.'

'Really – younger? I wasn't expecting that.'

'To tell the truth – neither was I.'

'And this is the effect of telomerase?'

'At passport checks,' I said, 'I try to look decrepit. Otherwise they'd never believe my date of birth.'

'How extraordinary.'

'We are still at an early stage. I am writing an observation paper. And soon I will publish an article in *Genome* magazine. It is my duty, of course.'

'Gene therapy,' he said, 'has been around for some time. No one knows what marvels may soon become possible. What you are doing – your experiment – is completely new.'

'Yes – it sounds like science fiction. But it is not, of course.' I felt strong and buoyant. 'I am flesh and blood, like all of us. I am alive, and healthier than ever.'

'Is telomerase the secret of immortality?'

'Perhaps. At least it stops one growing old.'

'You must be so proud. To be creating something that humans have always dreamed about. The universal dream. Not to mention, of course, a Nobel for yourself.'

'That is immaterial.'

◆◆

'Let's go out,' I said. 'I'd like to show you my domain.'

'Certainly.'

I took the bottle and the glasses and led him to the door.

'I mustn't forget this!' said the journalist, picking up the recording machine.

Outside the sky had clouded over. It was still windy, but not cold.

'Let's go over there,' I said, pointing to the line of stones at the edge of the drop. 'We can sit down, and continue our conversation.'

I poured a full shot of wine for each of us, and we clinked glasses. It was quite comfortable, sitting on the stones. The man placed the little recorder on the ground between us.

'Before we go any further,' he said, 'may I offer you some remuneration for this interview?' He had to speak loudly; the wind covered our words.

I considered this. If I asked for an exorbitant sum, the man would probably refuse. But he would write an article anyway, a hostile article.

So I said, 'One hundred euros would be fine.'

'I am sure *Le Monde* would be happy with that.'

'Thank you.'

'I'll get it sent to you.'

'In the meantime – may I take a picture? For the article. A picture of you in your mountain den?'

'You may.'

The man opened his bag and took out a small camera.

I stood up and posed. He took several pictures, and each time there was a bright flash.

This gave me an idea. I felt in my pocket; my torch was there.

The man returned the camera to his bag, which he held tight as if afraid of letting go. The canvas straps hung down.

'What about you?' I said. 'Would you dare to do what I am doing?'

The man smiled. 'I'm not as brave as you. But I might, I suppose. If I was in your position.'

'But even if you were not? Wouldn't you like to remain young, for ever?'

'Who wouldn't?'

'It turns out to be easier than we thought.'

'Could you tell me a little more? How did the idea first occur to you?'

'You will have to wait, I'm afraid. First, I must publish the results in a professional magazine.'

'Of course. I'm not expecting you to reveal your secrets. But I believe you consider the ageing process to be merely a kind of disease, curable with the correct medicine. Is that right?'

'Yes,' I replied. 'A disease like any other. A malfunction.'

'And you have found a cure?'

I ignored his question.

'Listen,' I said. 'Can you hear that?'

Far below, the river was roaring.

'Is it water?'

'Yes. My river. I go for a swim every morning, even in winter. One of the advantages of our treatment. You become so young and fit that you hardly feel the cold.'

I took the torch from my pocket, and switched it on. I directed the light towards the precipice.

'Come with me,' I said. 'I will show you.'

I took him to the edge.

'All this,' I said, with a sweep of my arm, 'evolved millions of years ago. Little by little. Can you imagine that time-scale?'

'Magnificent,' he said. 'I understand your attraction to this place.'

'For me, past and present are one.'

'How interesting.'

'I live in the present moment.'

'You are lucky.'

I winked at him. 'Are you envious?'

'Perhaps a bit.'

I heard the river below. It was swollen by the recent rain.

'Time,' I said, 'is no longer a stream that rushes by.'

'We are told the secret of happiness is to live in the present.'

'An impossibility – for ordinary people.'

The man nodded.

Then he said, 'But what is good? What is better? Can we really know?'

He bowed his head. And I almost felt sorry for him. He stood there, staring at the ground, bereft, ignorant. What is good? What is better? Old Victor would have tried to console him, put his arm round his shoulders, spoken encouragingly, even accompanied him back to the village. But I could do none of this.

Eventually I said, 'We are both grown-up people. We have a certain experience of life. You can understand what a relief it is to talk about my situation.'

'Of course,' he said. 'I am grateful. It must be a burden to remain silent about something so important—'

But it was too late. He lifted his head and I shone the torch beam full in his face.

'Yes,' I said. 'You understand my predicament.'

I saw him clearly in the powerful beam. A vigorous man, intent on making a good career. He hunched over; the sole of one dirty trainer scraped loose, his hand went up trying to protect his eyes. The light really was blinding. It was an effective high-tech torch that came with the Cayman.

'Don't do that,' he said. 'Please.'

His glass clattered to the ground. I saw the red wine spilling out, darkening the soil.

Just behind him was one last stone, close to the edge.

'Give that to me,' I said, pointing to his bag. 'You might trip over the straps. Or you might drop it and damage the camera.'

The word 'drop' gave me some pleasure. I snatched the bag from his hands, which were trembling slightly.

'Thank you,' I said.

My own hand was quite steady, as I held the torch. I was grinning, but he couldn't see that.

I advanced firmly, driving the light towards him. He backed away, perilously close to the edge. I could turn off the torch, that was still a possibility. Or, with a sensible survival instinct, he could simply step to one side.

But instead, mesmerised by the beam, he just went on stumbling backwards. Perhaps he really was tipsy. Behind him I saw the last stone.

I thought of saying, at the last moment: 'You're so dirty. Do go for a swim.' But the sound of my voice might bring him to his senses. So I just continued advancing.

What an unfortunate accident, I said to myself.

I could hardly have believed it would be so easy. Life and death so close. But I knew that already.

With predictable timing he tripped on the stone behind him, and fell straight over the edge. I heard the scuffle of his shoes against the dust. There was no cry, like in films. Just the silence of the mountain. It was a matter of seconds; as if nothing had happened.

I looked over the precipice. A mist lay across the river below like a sheet.

'Oh dear,' I said aloud. 'I told you it was dangerous to wander about up here.'

There was no trace of the man.

Immediately my attention was caught by something else.

There was a rustling in the hawthorn to my left; a black and white cat emerged and stopped in front of me. I shone the torch in its face; the cat hissed and arched its back. 'Little creature,' I said, putting out my hand. The cat's eyes were transparent like marbles. I moved slowly round, driving it towards the edge; the cat crept away, then crouched with its back to the precipice. I made a sudden rush at it, blasting the light into its eyes. Snarling the cat leapt to one side and disappeared into the bushes.

Taking a cotton handkerchief from my pocket I smoothed out the earth and wiped the stone the man had tripped over. I scattered a few twigs across the ground, and it all looked natural and undisturbed. Then I dropped the handkerchief over the cliff and watched it flutter down into the darkness. I picked up the recording machine and put it into the canvas bag.

A moment later I switched off the torch and set off on the path that leads higher up the mountain. The journalist's bag hung from my shoulder. My heart began to beat like a drum. It wasn't remorse or anxiety that was making my heart thud, but a kind of insatiable energy. It was appalling. But most exhilarating. My stride was fast and relentless, as if the death of the man had entered my blood and every cell in my body was firing with hellish power.

All the walks I had ever taken on the slopes of Castir seemed compressed into this one. As if I had always been in motion, crossing the mountain in all seasons, especially in winter, a pilgrim among the thorn bushes and chestnut trees coiling bare into the sky, and the cork oaks serenely clad in green.

I didn't go far. I returned to the Cayman, and opened the man's bag. I took out the recording machine and erased the interview. There were other things in it too: an address book, a cell phone and the camera. The phone was switched off; it would be impossible to locate. I closed the bag and put it in the space under the kitchen sink, with the cleaning materials. In the morning I would decide how to dispose of it.

Two days later I went to the village and bought the local paper. A mangled body had been found in the park at the base of a precipice. It appeared a man had fallen over the edge and smashed his head against the boulders below, where a river ran. Or it might have been suicide. The body was much damaged by the fall, and degraded by the water. The police were trying to establish the identity of the victim.

I read this with interest. Oddly enough, the memory of what had happened was already fading. It was almost as if it had nothing to do with me at all.

25

I persuaded Lucy to come out for a walk with me. The weather was mild; but it was already evening, which might have deterred her.

'I want to show you something,' I said.

I could see her hesitate, but then she agreed.

'You'll be interested,' I said.

We set off together, as so often before, up the mountain path. Nature was withdrawing, but there was still green on the trees.

We stopped and stood together, listening for animals.

A breeze began to blow; this I had been expecting, there was usually a wind higher up on the mountain. Above us the branches moved, and the leaves rustled as if streams of water were running around us.

We walked on, and night fell. My eyes were sharp, and I had no difficulty moving through the dark. Like a cat, I thought. It was my world; how often I roamed the hillside at night. I moved noiselessly; but behind me I heard Lucy's feet knocking against stones, and breaking dry sticks on the path.

The mountain was alive with sounds. Branches of trees rubbed and squeaked like human cries; and there were scurrying movements all around, as mice and other creatures ran away into the undergrowth.

Lucy fell behind me.

'Victor!' she called.

I stopped. 'I'm here,' I said.

I waited till she caught up, out of breath. Then I took her hand and smiled at her.

'It's the life of the mountain,' I said. 'More alive at night.'

We went on; I tried not to get too far ahead. And then I began to hear what I had been hoping for.

A lovely sound, still distant, trembled above the shimmer of leaves. Long drawn-out notes like siren calls joined together and pulsed with the movement of the breeze. I imagined Lucy's ears pricking, on full alert. The ears of a pianist.

The wind blew stronger and the singing grew clearer, one breathless note joined by another and then another.

'Please, Victor!' she said. 'Can we go down?'

I threw back my head and laughed silently.

'It's the trees singing,' I said. 'Are you afraid?'

'A little. Aren't you?'

I could see what she was thinking; that it was my own doing, Victor's double, the impostor, enchanting the mountainside.

I gripped her arm and led her on.

'Listen to it,' I said. 'The spirit of the wood.' I spoke gently, almost whispering into her ear.

I felt her body shaking, my little Lucy, her knees buckling.

'Let me go!'

But I held her firmly, my grip was like steel. I dragged her struggling a bit further and stopped. The unearthly whining was louder than ever. It was just above us.

'Look,' I said, pointing upwards. A darker shadow was clearly visible, high up in the branches.

'What is it?' she whispered.

I let her tremble a few moments more. Then I took the torch from my pocket and shone it up into the tree.

'Nature's siren,' I said.

'But what is it?' she whispered again, urgently.

Now she was clinging on to me with both hands.

'My own wild heart.'

'Stop it, Victor,' she said, trying to be calm. 'Tell me what it is.'

'A box,' I said.

'A box?'

'A wooden box.'

'But what is it?'

'An Aeolian harp.'

'What is that?'

'A box with strings.'

'A box with strings!'

The wind blew in a gust, and I heard three long wiry notes, whining and clashing. Tears came to my eyes, tears of joy. My eyes had been dry for so long. I laughed out loud.

'A wind harp,' I said. 'An ancient invention. Haven't you heard of it?'

She shook her head.

'Stop laughing!' she cried.

'Remember the piece by Chopin?'

'Who put it up there?'

'I did.'

'You wanted to frighten me!'

'I wanted to show you something.'

'You wanted to frighten me!'

Above us the singing box wailed in the breeze.

'I am sorry, Lucy,' I said. I heard my own voice; it sounded suddenly cracked and tired. 'I am sorry ...' I dropped the torch into the leaves at my feet.

I murmured, '"The Aeolian Harp", a piece by Chopin – isn't that right?'

Was it the old me?

She let go of my arms and tried to touch my cheek. But I slipped through her hands, and squatted on the ground, feeling for the torch. Then I stood up and shone the light under my chin.

'Shall I get it for you?'

She said nothing.

The next moment I was climbing the tree. With no difficulty I lifted myself from branch to branch, holding the torch in my teeth. High up I gripped the trunk with my legs and pulled at the box. It came clattering down and hit the ground beside Lucy, the strings twanging. She stepped away from it.

I slid down myself, feeling the grainy bark rubbing against my hands. I picked up the box and held it out to her. It was damp and heavy.

I said, 'Three wire strings resonating in the wind. That's all. Yet the effect ... enough to make you believe in goblins and spirits.'

She took the harp and plucked vaguely at the strings. Out of the wind it was lifeless and made no sound.

'The laws of physics,' I said. 'An Aeolian harp is an ancient thing. There's no special magic to it. Just a clever use of nature, an enhancement, a tweak – like the work we do. We genetic engineers are always looking for the right tweak ... and then,' I snapped my fingers, 'a deadly disease becomes something of the past. With a single dose, an injection, an inhalation ... certain death becomes life. For example.'

We turned and started to walk back. I matched my stride to hers. I took the heavy box from her and carried it under my arm.

'It's for you,' I said.

I reached out for her hand, but she pulled away.

'I don't want it,' she said.

'I'll keep it. But it's for you.'

26

The next day I phoned Lucy at the house.

'Can I come to dinner?' I asked.

'Do you really want to?'

'Yes.'

'All right,' she said.

I set out on foot from the Cayman, taking a short cut across the mountain. Everywhere the hawthorn was flaming with red berries. By this route, at my speed, the descent takes barely fifteen minutes. I passed the pool where I like to swim in the early morning, where the water is always cold, even at the height of summer. Colder still now, in autumn.

In my hand I carried a bottle of local wine. I intended to go first to the study and take my medication; it was time for my regular dose. But as I slipped quietly in the back door I came face to face with L. She was coming towards me carrying plates and a candle holder. A rich smell filled the house.

'I thought we'd eat out,' she said. 'It's still warm.'

I went into the kitchen, and saw washing-up to be done. I put on the rubber gloves, turned on the tap and waited for the hot water. There was a gurgle and small explosion as usual. On the stove sat the orange casserole with the chipped handle. I peered inside.

It was quite chilly on the terrace. L. put on a jumper and gave me a scarf. Damp air rose from the amphitheatre and moistened the plates.

'Season of mist and mellow fruitfulness,' I quoted, light-heartedly, from Keats.

'Close bosom-friend of the maturing sun … as if summer days will never cease …'

The words tripped off my tongue. I think I could have recited the whole poem.

'… like a gleaner …' I stopped.

'What is a gleaner?' I said.

Lucy shrugged.

The wind blew out the candle. We shivered simultaneously.

'The summer days *have* ceased,' I said.

We stared into the hollow amphitheatre. At night it looked like a cave. I thought of Prometheus in the mossy grotto, crawling across the rock.

'Rome,' I said.

'Yes?'

The scarf was scratching my neck.

'Remember?' I said. 'Remember, long ago, I took you to the hollow tree on Hampstead Heath?'

Lucy nodded.

I went on, 'We climbed inside. I took off the scarf you were wearing and tied it across your eyes, blindfolding you. Then with my scarf I covered my own eyes. We kissed like that, the first time, blindfold.'

It had been spring then, though cold. The tree was completely hollow and yet above it was alive with a canopy of new leaves. Inside, lots of people had written their names on the bark. One inscription affected us deeply. It said: 8.00 a.m., 1 August. With eternal love for my unborn child.

'Tell me about Rome,' you said. 'Did you stay long?'

'I spent a week there. While you were playing in Germany.'

'Yes, I remember.'

'I went to all our favourite places,' I said. 'It was just the same.'

You looked at me with surprise, I thought.

Your gaze was ironic: Rome? The same, of course.

But you're not the same.

I met your eyes. Not the same? But if I was exactly the same, after so many years, wouldn't that be frightening?

Your eyes accused me. No, Victor, that is not what I mean.

I know. But you're wrong. I am like everybody else. I want the same as everybody.

I said aloud, 'In the Villa Celimontana there was a statue I hadn't seen before. Prometheus. In fact Prometheus Unbound. He was crawling away from his chains. But I don't know the story, do you?'

Now you moved your chair and gazed into the amphitheatre. The moon rose. It was a long time, I wondered how long, since we had music there. I wondered how you played now, if it was the same as before. I wondered if you had any problems, any stiffness now in the joints of your fingers. For you are growing old. To play music with the wisdom of age and the perfect muscles of youth – wouldn't that be good? To be young later on – isn't that everybody's dream?

I said, 'I am, you know, like everybody else. I have the same desires, the same hopes.'

I laid my hands flat on the table. Both thumbs looked long. And the backs of the hands were hairy. But this happens naturally with the years.

The brown spots on the right had almost gone. Miraculous – the power of telomerase. Your hand, next to mine, was thin and withered, like a claw. I put my own under the table.

Rather to my surprise, I asked if one day, perhaps next year, you would like to play again, here in the amphitheatre. I told you – was it true? – that one of the happiest moments in my life was hearing you play Schubert's last sonata in this place. For life is a desert, I said, music the oasis.

With your eyes you said: would you like me to play again?

I answered out loud, 'What about next spring?'

You replied, 'Perhaps we could organise a proper season again. A new season.'

I was with you then, down from my cloud, flesh and blood

like you. Could I love you again, as I was now, with telomerase roaring through every cell in my body?

The thought came to me for the first time: immortality is dreary.

I said lightly, 'Sitting here with you, my darling, makes me realise beyond a doubt that immortality, really, is rather dreary.' We both laughed. I went on, 'The immortals, you know, were always falling in love with mortals, whom they found irresistibly attractive. They weren't much interested in loving their own kind.'

Under the table I rotated my wrist and there was a crunching sound. And suddenly my right hand seemed to be aching at the knuckles.

Meanwhile L. had remembered the Prometheus story: '… it was Hercules, I think, who cut his chains. And then—'

'Well then, don't crawl! Stand up!' I cried out, as if calling through space and time to P., a brother-in-arms.

Lucy laughed. She turned towards me affectionately, and I think nearly stroked my cheek: my brave Prometheus …

She was wearing, I saw, hanging from her neck, a little medallion I once gave her. On this medallion is a dark, shiny picture: a spindly tree with fresh green leaves rises from arid rocks. I once teased her that this was an image of our love, a love which however tender could survive the harshest conditions. At that time, like a teenager, I wanted to write her name everywhere. I engraved it with a nail on columns in Rome. And wherever I wrote it those four letters radiated light. LUCY.

Now I focused on the medallion and tried to find the tree. I looked hard for the romance I had once read into that quaint little scene. But all I could see was a black line against a satin sky.

Love, I said under my breath; the terror that makes us reach out in the night, and pour our hearts out, and beg to be understood.

'Do you remember,' I asked, 'the Roman street?'

She looked at me blankly.

'Yes,' I went on, 'the ancient Roman street under the church of St Giovanni and Paolo. We went there once. Amazingly well preserved, as if the inhabitants had just moved out. We took off our shoes and walked over the mosaic floors just like the people of so long ago.'

She smiled. 'Yes I remember – we were happy, weren't we?'

The amphitheatre shone like slate in the moonlight. Beyond I could see a row of bushes and then the looming mountain.

Darkness holds no terrors for me. There are no witches, no spirits to make me curl up and clamp shut my eyes. The moon is dead rock, a star is a ball of gas, a heart is a beating muscle. Behind everything is the huge cold mystery, and I am not afraid of that either. The mystery is with me all the time, and I am enthralled by it.

Under the table, where I had been half unconsciously massaging my knuckles, Lucy touched my hand. She was trying to say that although I have become monstrous she still wanted to try and remember me from the old days. I felt her breath on my cheek.

Her hand scratched like a dry twig against mine. I suddenly squeezed it so hard that she cried out in pain. At the same time I imagined a whole orchestra in the amphitheatre, splitting the air like an explosion. I let go her hand.

'Could we get an orchestra in there?'

'An orchestra!'

'Yes, why not?'

I still had to take my dose. I don't like delaying it, even by a half-day.

Lucy said, 'Is there something I can do? Is there some way I can help you, Victor?'

It is of course to be expected that she sees me as a poor mixed-up case, a kind of alarming invalid.

I replied, 'Sometimes it is as though I am clearing up a house, the house of a person dead, gone, and I come across old letters, notes, diaries, address books, and photograph albums, pictures that I myself have carefully stuck in place, deceptive as photographs are ... you could help me with that, perhaps.'

'I'm not sure I understand you.'

'And then when that's done we could think again.'

'By the way, people have been looking for you.'

'Not again.'

'I usually send them away. They are journalists.'

'Thank you.'

'One was here today. From the *New York Times*. He said he'll come back.'

'Oh well. I'll talk to him.'

'I'm afraid one of them caught me off guard. A Frenchman. I mentioned the camper van on the mountain.'

'It doesn't matter.'

'Did he come to see you?'

'No, no one came.'

She got up and went into the house. When she returned she was carrying a tartan rug. She sat down beside me and pulled the rug over our legs.

'I was cold and you must have been too,' she said.

◆◆

I drew the rug over my knees, feeling its roughness, and I had a Proustian flash. I remembered the day I bought this rug, and one other, in John Lewis. It was only about two months ago.

What would have happened to Proust if telo had existed in his day? Would he have leapt at the chance to recover his youth and his life, ill as he was, haunted by time?

'I remember buying this rug,' I said to Lucy. As if turning back the pages of an album, I could see myself walking in John Lewis with the two rugs I had just bought, through the haberdashery section.

And there I saw an old lady, a little bowed, choosing thread. I recognised her immediately, from behind; the angle of her body, leaning a little to the left, and her right foot, turning out.

'I saw my sister Pauline,' I said.

I had not seen Pauline for a long time, I am not sure how long; she lives in Wales and hardly ever comes to London. She lives in a small village near the coast, with the woman she loves, and teaches the cello – she has quite a reputation there, I believe, and sometimes gives concerts in local churches and village halls. She is a good musician, and she could, I am sure, have had a fine career – but instead she prefers to live quietly in a cottage with Rosie and two Dalmatians.

I rubbed the rug on my legs between thumb and forefinger, to bring back the memory more sharply.

The wool was rough and fibrous. I could almost feel the atoms themselves, and the whirling electrons inside them bonding with other whirling electrons; sometimes I am suddenly aware of all this, the cosmic dance – it is so exhilarating.

You realise that everything is quite incomprehensible; whoever you are, you can only wonder. It makes you feel humble. Like the American astronauts who have been to the moon; there are only nine of them, out of a world population of seven billion, but they are modest people, not vain or arrogant – because they have seen something so much bigger.

'You saw Pauline in John Lewis?' said Lucy.

'Yes,' I said. 'After so long.'

I stood beside Pauline, that time, quite close, and pretended to be also searching through needles and cotton spools, and waited for her to look up. After a while she looked straight at me, and I was moved; I saw not an old dowdy woman, but my vibrant youthful sister. I was just about to take her in my arms when she turned away. A shiver ran up my spine; she had not recognised her brother. And yet surely I looked *more* like me, more like the boy she had always known?

I followed Pauline as she hobbled from counter to counter, sampling threads and materials. Her movements were laboured, and I could see that her knuckles were swollen with arthritis. I followed her around John Lewis and everything seemed antiquated, escalators and lifts and cash tills, and even the goods themselves, as if all these things had become obsolete.

I lost sight of Pauline for a bit, as I became distracted by the decaying faces wobbling past, for which I felt some compassion, but also, to tell the truth, some repulsion. Eventually I saw her again fumbling in her purse at the cash desk; the old lesbian, I thought, and wondered if her moustache was growing. At the same time I remembered discovering, all those years ago, that she loved her own sex, and how she became lit up and full of energy when she was visited dying by the girl she loved, and began, from that moment, to recover from leukaemia.

I could see Pauline was about to turn towards me and I called her name. Then she turned, a big smile on her face, and we embraced. I went on talking, mumbling expressions of delight, aware that my voice had not changed, and that was how she knew me, afraid that if I stopped speaking she would see me once again as a stranger.

We went to the café, and I asked her about her life, about her friend Rosie and the cello; I talked incessantly, showed interest in the details of her country life, and yet I knew, all the time, that I was playing a role.

Pauline looked at me with tears in her eyes, and I lowered mine out of fear, or shame, or some other emotion, knowing in advance what she was about to say; and she said it: 'Victor, you look so amazingly well and young. How do you do it? You must be very happy. I am also content, and yet I have grown old. Rosie, you know, is so much younger than me ... but the wonderful thing is – and it is extraordinary, isn't it? – that she doesn't mind.'

My sister! I knew how much I have always loved her, admired her, indeed she has been for me a model of courage, of independence, and also of constancy. It seemed to me that it was perhaps above all because of her, Pauline, because of her example, that I had the strength, the daring, to try telo, to follow it through, to be the first.

I knew all this, and was pleased to see her; but I didn't feel much.

I said, 'Pauline, I want to tell you that all my life you have been an inspiration to me. I have followed your example.'

She looked at me with tender concern, waiting for me to continue.

What was it, I thought, this tender concern, what exactly was happening to her lips, her cheeks, the muscles round her eyes? I watched her closely. She tilted her head to the left, lowered it, and was looking up at me with one eyebrow raised and the other squashed down. The head looked unsteady, and it occurred to me that if she tilted it a little more it might come off and roll onto the tea table.

The face, with its concentration of features slightly askew, like a busy traffic junction, was small and round and seemed separate from the rest. I stared at my dear sister, and then, quite clearly, I saw her head lying as if exhausted against a tea cup on the table. It was still squinting at me from one eye.

I said, 'How are the Dalmatians?'

The floppy lips moved and said in the sweetest voice: 'Fine. Victor darling, my little brother, I've always adored you and admired you so much. Don't let's allow so much time to go by.'

When she spoke her face came together. I blinked and saw my sister again.

'How is Lucy?' she asked.

'Oh she's very well,' I replied.

'And you?' The concern was there again; and apprehension.

A tiny flush of emotion came to my eyes. I looked at my watch and stood up.

'Good heavens – I almost forgot! I have an appointment … one day, Pauline, I will tell you – I've got so much to tell you … a lot has happened to me.'

We embraced quickly and I left her sitting at the table.

I said to Lucy, 'And I haven't seen her since. You see I was ashamed – of looking so young … that's what's so hard to take, I understand, it must seem ridiculous.'

'But how young are you, actually?' she asked in a small, bemused voice.

Both of us almost laughed. In normal circumstances it would have been funny, very funny, and the way we were talking now was almost normal, it was almost as if we were reminiscing, recalling an odd interlude in our lives, long past.

But the seconds passed and it was no longer funny. I could think of no answer to her question. As I looked at her she seemed to zoom away, far away ... I put out a hand to stop her, but she didn't take it.

Once again, like strangers, we had nothing to say to each other.

◆◆

I didn't like this silence.

So I said, 'Do you remember, after my cancer operation we went to a concert with MM? It was Mahler. *The Song of the Earth.*'

This piece of music, 'The Farewell', now came back to me so clearly that I began to hum it. Surprisingly the words came back too – in German, a language I hardly know. My memory was phenomenal. There they were, the words, and I sang them, in a kind of croak:

'*Die liebe Erde alluberall bluht auf
im Lenze und grunt aufs neu!
Alluberall und ewig blauen
licht die Fernen!
Ewig ... ewig ...*'

'I'm sorry,' I said, apologising for my tuneless groaning.

All the same, I couldn't help translating them, for Lucy's benefit:

'The dear Earth everywhere blossoms forth
in Spring and turns green anew!
Everywhere, for ever blue

glows the distant horizon!

For ever ... for ever ...'

And that, I realised, that's what I wanted to hear in the amphitheatre.

Was my love of music returning?

'I doubt it,' I said softly to myself.

Lucy didn't seem to hear. 'Where did you get that from?' she asked. 'Those words?'

'From the programme. And perhaps,' I suggested, 'you could play a concerto in the first half?'

Lucy said nothing.

'What do you think?' I went on. 'Remember how often we listened to the old recording with Kathleen Ferrier? *The Song of the Earth?*'

And, yes, I seemed to hear it now; as I gazed at the shadowy theatre and the starry vault, those last repeated notes, the endless farewell, echoing like the cry of a departing spirit across the empty, empty space, for ever ... Yet, although I imagined the music in the silent amphitheatre, and Lucy playing too, it was as if I myself wasn't there.

I reached out for L, and there was a click in my shoulder and a sharp pain up the arm; my other hand shot to my neck and chin, expecting to find there a sudden growth of loose skin like a turkey.

But there wasn't; my neck was smooth as alabaster.

You stood up and began clearing things off the table. I pushed back my chair with a clatter, ran up to you and made a crazy face.

You screamed.

Now this scream gave me some pleasure, so I just stood still, without changing my expression. You looked lovely, standing there on the terrace with the dishes.

You screamed again. I took a step closer, grimacing madly. And then I could no longer control it. My face burst into movement, as if frenzied ants were attacking me. You dropped a plate and it shattered on the tiles. Suddenly we were like two animals let out of their cages.

'Go away!' you said.

I froze, like Prometheus.

'I don't want you!' you cried. 'How could I?' Pause. 'I don't want you now, and *even before* … yes, even before, Victor, when you thought you understood me so well, when you thought I was so happy and you went on and on about our love and how we were the happiest couple … you put me on a pedestal, your shy little pianist, you showed me off, I brought tears to your eyes, didn't I? You were sentimental, Victor. But did you see me, did you ever really *see* me? Oh no – you wanted me your way, and when I wouldn't play the game, when I wasn't that delicate little creature that you wanted, you got angry. You were often impatient, remember? And I thought it was my fault, there was something wrong with me … I believed you, I was so much younger than you … And sex – I felt guilty about that too, because you were so pleased with yourself … You see I have never been a pure little nymph who lives for music.'

Now she brought her face surprisingly close to mine. I wondered if, despite everything, she was suddenly going to kiss me.

'Then, Victor … then you started this experiment, and you didn't even tell me.' Her voice dropped to a whisper, and there was something in her eyes I had never seen before – disgust. 'You started this genetic nightmare which was going to change your life, *our* lives, utterly, and you didn't even tell me, you didn't consult me, you didn't ask me … why? Because you were frightened what I would say? I don't think so. You didn't tell me because it didn't occur to you. You thought it was none of my business.'

I stared at her. Even now, it was as if I was the magician, putting the words into her mouth.

'And I know,' she said, 'I know perfectly well – you haven't given it up. You are still taking the drug.'

I looked at her with my magnetic gaze. And I saw the

strangeness in her eyes, the elusiveness which had once so drawn me.

She said, 'Love is a selfish thing, don't you think?' They could have been my own words.

I replied coolly, 'Who can say what is selfish and what isn't, in love?'

She went on, 'I have to tell you, Victor. I haven't been faithful to you.' Pause. 'And I'm not talking about now. I'm talking about before.' She said this without a quiver, with no fear of my reaction, looking me straight in the eye. 'And not just once. Are you surprised? Did you come with me on my concert tours? I needed it. I needed you – and, yes, I needed *others* ... does that surprise you?'

She was trying to make me jealous.

'Did you wonder,' she said, 'why I so often went to Germany, why I played in so many small towns and villages in that country, why I stayed so long? Did it occur to you? Well, now I'm telling you. Yes, it was Niko. Yes, I did sleep with him. More than once.' She stared at me. 'When I was moody and sulky you took no notice and put it down to my "artistic nature". But it wasn't that. It was because I didn't know what to do. Whether to stay with you or leave you. You never guessed, of course. Yes, I felt bad about it. I was supposed to be the happy wife, obsessed by her piano. But I wasn't. I'm sorry to have to tell you this. But perhaps now it suits you. Perhaps now you don't mind. Before, there was something in your expression, the way you looked at me, that brought me back. And I admired you. I thought, it ought to be possible, it must be possible.'

I said, 'Naturally you don't see that now. My face is a mask, hard and shiny.'

'I have tried, Victor. I have tried hard.'

She sighed. During all this her hands had been tightly clenched together. Now she opened them.

She said in a different voice, 'Actually, I haven't had many lovers. Perhaps I should have – but it's been mainly in my head.'

She piled the dishes on top of each other, and went on, 'I don't want to hold you back, Victor. I'm telling you, you don't have to worry about me. Do what you have to. You're a scientist, after all. I shall be all right. Yes, I have loved you, I loved you a lot ... but now – follow your star.'

Then she walked into the house with the dishes.

27

I climbed down from the terrace and went out through the amphitheatre. I took the track and began to mount the hill. A mist was forming and the ground was damp. There was no wind at all, not even a breeze. All was muffled. I went up past the car park. The path became muddy and steep, the fog thicker. I went on. I couldn't hear the river, the fog seemed to have absorbed it like blotting paper. I passed the Cayman and continued up.

The path came to an end and I crossed the hillside directly. You have to be careful in the dark. It is easy to trip and catch your foot in the scrub or a rabbit hole. But my legs were working fine, and my vision was clear. Strange, I thought, the way one moment you have everything, the next nothing. But did that matter now?

I saw Luc again, the bright schoolboy on the train to Rome, dancing in his socks on the frozen platform. He turned back and waved, just as the train was moving off. And I waved too, at the window. Where were his shoes now?

I made my way slowly and carefully through the fog, still climbing. Beside me walked the beast of solitude, my beast. MM said we are driven to seek solace beyond ourselves, the self alone is never enough. The beast of solitude, I said. My words were immediately swallowed up, in the air thick like a shroud. Poor beast, I said dramatically.

Then I stumbled against something and stopped.

At my feet was a dead fox. It lay on its back, the fur intact, the belly round and full. But the snout, the ears and the eyes were seething with maggots. And the tail. Slowly, with the movement of the maggots, the tail wagged back and forth. This was life, not death. I laughed. Yes, life.

Who else was there, I thought, apart from Niko?

Something was nagging at me; I hadn't taken my medicine.

On the ground the maggots swarmed over one another, feeding and fattening, and their numbers seemed to increase each moment in a breeding frenzy. Their glowing whiteness lit the ground like a lamp. The fox squirmed, its stomach heaved, as if alive. And so it was. The fox was alive.

I am free, I said aloud. My Lucy has flown away.

Then it hit me.

She has left me.

The years fell away; I became old. My skin crumpled, my hair grew white and thin, my knees buckled.

Or so it seemed.

I shouted, 'I love you, Lucy!'

This I cried, theatrically, to the wild world around me, but it was no less true for that.

For I was mistaken; I did not make you happy.

But could I, old and bowed, could I try again? You are my love – I will never forget it again! I would give up telomerase. I would do all in my power, everything conceivable, for the rest of my life, to win you back. I will give it up! I promise. And then perhaps could I, if you let me, could I at last make you happy?

From far away, through the mist, I heard a sound.

It was a low hoarse sound, which rose to a whining pitch, and broke off. There was silence; then it started again. A moment later came an answering call; and another, and another. Now, all around me, the mountain vibrated with desolate cries, like the bellowing of primeval horns. Close by, a roar broke out and vaguely I saw a big shape and a crest of moving branches. And through the thick cold air came a sour, musky smell.

It was the deer. I had never heard so many; my blood throbbed and the music coursed through me, a symphony in rut, wild straining voices of pain and desire. And I too, like a madman, raised my head and bellowed; I roared with the stags, we roared together. Then, as a storm sweeps by in a tumult, the sounds became fainter and fainter, echoing across the distance, and gradually fell silent, until they disappeared completely and the mountain was once again hushed.

The mist broke into threads and I saw the stars, oh so far away.

I began to run, to rush across the hillside, back to the path, past the Cayman and the cliff where I had driven the journalist to his death, down to the river where he had smashed against the boulders, alongside the river as it plunges into the valley, the limpid pools where I bathed every day, out onto the wider track towards the village; and all the way, one word throbbed through me: Alone.

In an instant I was at the house.

I fumbled with the keys, my hands shaking, all the locks were drawn. At last the door opened. In the pitch dark I flew up the stairs. I knew where I was going: to our bedroom.

But something held me back. On the first floor I stopped. My feet were glued to the landing.

What are you doing? I said to myself.

I couldn't help it; it was time.

I ran into the study without closing the door. The refrigerator glowed white. Trembling I unlocked it, grabbed an inhaler and threw myself into the leather chair. Putting the nozzle to my mouth, I paused, I held my breath. Titanium, rare metal … Prometheus, a Titan? I pressed the catch.

Indescribably lovely the eucalyptus vapour curled across my tongue; I drew it deeply down. I lay back in the chair and laughed quietly.

Alive!

I pressed the catch again. My heartbeat quickened, I closed my eyes. Fifteen counts later I pressed the catch for the third time. I was at peace. I was afloat.

It seemed that I had always been there, in that chair by the window, and all the rest, all the rest of everything, was nothing but a backdrop. Opening my eyes I saw the room clearly; all looked small and remote, the furniture, the desk and the books – only the refrigerator was real. I was soaring above the world, and it shone at my feet; I could encompass it all. How strange, how blissful to be alive – to be alive like this!

Snapshots poured through my head: Andres, the secret textbook, the blotched pictures of the frogs' skin. And then my mother's radiant face.

Tell me – was it him? You died without telling me … Was he really my father? Or was it only your wish?

I said: I understand, I forgive you.

After all, it hardly mattered now; for I was Everyman.

Then I saw my mother in her decline, her confusion, sighing to herself. Small and puzzled I heard her voice, saying: now, I mustn't put the butter into the marmalade. The butter must go on my toast; and then comes the marmalade. But although I know this is the right thing to do, I always put the butter into the marmalade pot. I can't help myself.

I put the inhaler back into the fridge, locked it, and came onto the landing.

I thought: I've done it. Now I would slip out and go back to the van.

But instead I began to climb the stairs. Carefully I avoided two that creaked. As I went up I felt something changing. With each step something began to drain away from me.

28

Very quietly I opened the door to our bedroom. Lucy lay under the duvet, her face turned to the wall. On the bedside table was the lamp we had once brought back from Rome, a pink marble Pantheon complete with hole in the roof.

I sat down on the little chair beside the bed. The fingers of her right hand twitched.

Don't panic, I whispered.

I waited till I could hear her regular breathing. I could see the back of her head, her long hair which had been unevenly dyed. Occasionally she muttered something, as if dreaming.

In a whisper I said: I expected to be full of lust like a young man.

I got up and went to the window. A band of light lay across the horizon, although it was too early for dawn. I turned back to the body on the bed. I looked for signs of breathing. What separates life from death?

Rome, I whispered, do you remember? I began to pace uncomfortably about the room.

Trying to remain calm I spoke to myself: the fact is, we are a complicated bunch of molecules ... but that is all we are and every bit of us obeys the laws of chemistry. Evolution is a hit and miss affair. To think we are perfect as evolution has made us is sheer stupidity. Before we did not have the necessary knowledge ... So we invented a spiritual path based on frustration and suffering. Nietzsche was the first philosopher to refuse these empty consolations.

Now in some agitation I again sat down on the chair beside the bed. I bent over Lucy and looked at her face.

I said in a whisper: I am the first to do it, that is all. In the future I will be remembered as a benefactor. Do you understand that?

I went on: as for love, it depends on so little, don't you agree, nothing is more fragile; now I see it clearly, yet it is strange, don't you think, that everything we believe matters, the sense that life is worth living or not, should hang by a thread?

Once again I stood up, feeling restless, and walked around the room as silently as I could, touching the chair, the walls, the table. I came to a halt against the window and pressed the glass hard and I thought it might break. Outside there was a screeching of birds. Moonlight entered.

I said: all is lost, or all is gained, life is right, or life is wrong – and nothing but a hair's breadth divides one from the other.

I looked into the night, the amphitheatre and the rock face.

My lips against the glass, I muttered inaudibly: after all, so little separates wanting to kill someone from wanting to love them. How often one murders people in one's thoughts, especially the ones we love most. But why?

We want to punish them.

I closed my eyes and heard the voices of the rutting stags, one after the other. Their yearning symphony sent shivers up my spine, yet it soothed me, taking me out of the little room, back to the clinging mountain and the mist.

And I saw the amphitheatre as if lit by candles, the candles we used to place in glass jars at the end of each row on concert nights. The summer twilight is slow, the candle flames hardly visible until the performance is under way. Then the faces glow, some listen eyes closed, others stare towards you, Lucy, as you play, all of them, even the oldest, like children, turned by music once again into children. I see the theatre full of dim faces, all turned towards you, and you are playing, you are in the heart of Schubert's last sonata, a small lamp beside the piano, at the end of the slow movement where Schubert writes, very softly, as soft as possible, then, even softer – and there in the depths of silence, the greatest longing, the abyss opens.

Yes, I remembered that.

I opened my eyes, and there was nothing there; just the night and the moon.

I stood full against the window, darkening the room, a bat with wings outstretched. Touching, I thought, that bats should fill us with such horror. A bat, mammal like me, same DNA in its cells, just a shuffle of the pack.

I turned and moved towards you, my abundant hair leapt forward. You looked dishevelled. Your right leg lay exposed. Damp strands of hair covered your face. I stared at your calf, your thigh which ran under the quilt. The heat of your body filled the room like a gas. The old world – remember? For I needed it now, urgently. I saw the alleyways of your blood, irrigating and warming you like a furnace. The alleys of Rome, the Forum, the dried blood bricks, there we were happy, do you remember?

I moved from the window and stood beside you.

I said: And the Roman street? Deep below the church the ancient street? Remember the mosaic floors? Ducks, geese, fish, wild boar – remember? We ran across them in our socks, we laughed, we wanted to stay all night? We spoke in whispers, we didn't want to disturb the ghosts … and the young woman on the wall, crossing the river to the other side?

I don't know what it was about this and about everything in the world that now suddenly seemed so devastating: something that made me put my knuckles between my teeth and bite till there was blood on my tongue. I said out loud, 'And there the momentary glory of your blooming–'

Now I was on the bed, but didn't touch her. I held out my hand above her face. I could feel her breath, still, even; it moistened the palm of my hand.

I whispered: a billion breaths. Regular lifespan.

How many breaths had she taken?

Beside her head was a second pillow, puffed and full. It too seemed to breathe, slowly inflating and deflating. I counted the breaths of the pillow.

My lips cracked open, I felt the corners stretching. I realised: I was smiling.

I saw my hand as it hovered above her nose and mouth. Only an inch between her face and me. The fingers were splayed, the tendons rigid, the knuckles white. The last phalange turned down like a talon.

Then she woke. Rapidly, deftly, she moved across the bed. She sat up and turned towards me. Her eyes glinted, hard as stone.

'Who are you?' she said.

'Your husband.'

'If you could see yourself ...'

'I know what I look like.'

'Go away.'

'Touch me,' I said. For I wanted it desperately. 'Please touch me.'

The next moment she was off the bed. Her hand shot out and she snatched something from the table: her phone.

She murmured, 'I must go to the bathroom.'

She locked the door of the bathroom, and I saw the light come on round the edges. Then I heard her voice, saying into the phone, 'Police? Could you come quickly. There's an intruder in my house.'

I'm back here now, in the Cayman. I left immediately.

I'm not going to put on the light, I don't need to.

I recovered as I went up the hillside.

I'm going to stop now and pull out my bunk.

I've got MM's face in my mind, his big teeth and baby eyes – I want to laugh, he looks so comical – and he's repeating the old refrain: 'Don't forget it's love that matters, Victory! Whatever happens, don't forget. You know that.'

Of course I Victor in my youth believed entirely in love, there was nothing else of much importance.

The wind harp lies against the wall. She never took it. The wood is thick and warped. The strings rusty.

I have a little candle in a red glass which I sometimes keep burning all night. Once in Italy I slept in a peasant's house with a candle like this in a red glass which burned all night in front of an icon. And, even though it was a light, it seemed to make the room darker.

I am up to date with my diary. I'm relieved to have got it all down.

Words after all are company; even those you write yourself.

POSTSCRIPT

Jay Elliot, Legal and Commercial Director, writes:

Dear colleagues,

I enclose, for your personal perusal, a memoir written by Victor Zimmerman, founder of the Zimmerman research laboratory in Archway, London.

This laboratory was the forerunner of our present company, Zimmerman Azorin.

As you are aware, the anti-ageing drug SARMELOT, manufactured by us, has been available for general use for several years. Before manufacture, extensive safety tests were conducted on human subjects, according to the prescribed rules; and no negative side effects were registered. As a result, a licence to produce the drug was granted.

Recently, the enclosed memoir has come to light.

A number of years have passed since Dr Zimmerman wrote these pages.

His death occurred, we believe, soon after he completed the last entry. Many of you know that Dr Zimmerman's lifeless body was discovered in the river that runs through the nature reserve at Castir, in the province of Jaen, Spain. He died from a blow to the back of his head, after a fall from the clifftop above.

Dr Zimmerman had been living in a camper van which was parked at a spot some hundred and fifty metres above a vertical drop to the aforementioned river. It is thought that he often walked on the Castir hillside at night, despite the known dangers of the terrain.

All the same, it is somewhat surprising that Dr Zimmerman, who knew the hillside and its pitfalls so well, should have accidentally fallen to his death. We cannot refute, for sure, the possibility that he ended his life on purpose – despite his clear determination to prolong his existence indefinitely.

Dr Zimmerman's unexpected demise was considered a serious loss to medical research. No autopsy was performed on the body, and his death was registered as accidental. This was considered satisfactory by his widow.

Mrs Zimmerman, Lucy, a concert pianist, is now also recently deceased. She stated, at the time of her husband's death, that she was estranged from Dr Zimmerman, and was living separately in the village of Castir.

Dr Mikhail Makarevich, referred to in the memoir as MM, was thought to have been in the area at the time. However, we have no precise information on this. He was not mentioned in the report on Dr Zimmerman's death. He too is now deceased.

The camper van, where Dr Zimmerman had been living, was left empty in its place on the Castir mountain. It was eventually retrieved by the local Council, and refashioned into a kiosk. It is now permanently stationed at the entrance to the Reserve, and sells souvenirs to visiting tourists.

After her husband's demise, Mrs Zimmerman and Dr Makarevich discovered the enclosed memoir among Dr Zimmerman's possessions. Other items too were found, in particular a small rucksack containing personal effects, including a camera and recording machine, both of which were degraded and non-functional.

After careful editing, Dr Zimmerman's manuscript was eventually published in *Genome*, a specialised journal.

The treatment was then at an early stage, and Dr Zimmerman's account never reached a wider public. However, recently rumours have been circulating, inaccurate as rumours tend to be, and I judge it correct to pass on Dr Zimmerman's document, unabridged, to senior colleagues.

Before their deaths, Mrs Zimmerman and Dr Makarevich expressed, in old age, a personal interest in trying out life-prolonging medication. However our drug SARMELOT was not yet ready, and both decided, with regret, that they would not take the risk of subjecting themselves to a potentially dangerous and unapproved treatment. Only Dr Zimmerman had so far experimented with a telomerase-based intervention; and his was not an example they wished to follow.

If we were to judge the effects of anti-ageing medication from the experience of reading Dr Zimmerman's text, our conclusions might well be negative. None of us would want to promote the kind of human being that Dr Zimmerman became, nor condone his behaviour.

However, times have changed.

Dr Zimmerman himself was in no doubt that the ageing process should be treated as a malfunction; in other words a disease. The drug he invented has gone through radical transformation, and SARMELOT is the result.

As you are aware, this medication is in widespread use, and demand is high.

Whatever your opinion after reading Dr Zimmerman's memoir, please remember that it was written in a different age. 'Telo', as he calls it, was a drug in its infancy. Dr Zimmerman was the only person alive experimenting with 'telo'; and he was fully aware of the dangers of his infant drug. He referred to any difficulties he encountered as 'teething problems'.

'Telo' bears little relation to our present sophisticated creation. Once again may I remind you that SARMELOT has successfully passed all safety tests, and our company was granted an exclusive licence to produce, by the official authorities.

I enclose the memoir, therefore, for your private perusal, out of a sense of duty. It is, as you will see, a curiosity; of little relevance to our current activities.

I see no point, no advantage, in making the memoir generally available to the public at this time. I consider it, above all, of historical interest; an addition to the literature we have already received on the subject.

I intend to store it in an appropriate file in the archives of our company.

Jay Eliot CBE

ACKNOWLEDGEMENTS

I would like to thank my agent, Antony Topping, for his remarkable persistence and belief in this book, and for his precious suggestions without which *Unbound* would never have achieved its present form. The brilliant surgeon, Stephen Hamilton, gave me invaluable information on medical research and patenting issues. My companion, Manel Guell, has been a constant support, and his artistic judgement has contributed greatly to the final version of the book. There are many others whose unflagging encouragement has helped and sustained me throughout; I would like to mention in particular Sasha McGlashan, Nigel Atkinson, Max Porter, Helen Francis, Ariane Bankes, Catarina Albano, Dominique Mols, Michael Shak. This short, and certainly incomplete, list must also include Joe Harper, Angeline Rothermundt and Piers Russell-Cobb at my publisher, Arcadia Books, and Cassie Lawrence and Lucy Dundas at Flint PR. I am deeply grateful for their unfailing courtesy and irreproachable professionalism. I am lucky indeed to have had such a dedicated team working on my behalf.